# "So, you're preg

The question sounded so incredibly stupid to his own ears. Of course Samantha was pregnant. If the breeze hadn't been billowing her loose dress around her before, he would have noticed that fact right away.

She let out a deep sigh and nodded. "Yes."

"Why didn't you tell me before?"

Samantha stared out at the horizon, the stinging in her eyes uncomfortable, but nothing compared to having Nick this close. She'd been in turmoil over how to tell him about the child.

*"Nick, I'm having your baby."* That sounded direct and right, but something inside her wouldn't let her say the words.

She'd practiced telling him enough, long into the empty nights. She'd rehearsed what to say, what not to say, what to do. But none of that mattered now. Her heart was pounding and her stomach was in knots. Nothing was ever simple with Nick.

Dear Reader,

May is the perfect month to stop and smell the roses, and while you're at it, take some time for yourself and indulge your romantic fantasies! Here at Harlequin American Romance, we've got four brand-new stories, picked specially for *your* reading pleasure.

Sparks fly once more as Charlotte Maclay continues her wild and wonderful CAUGHT WITH A COWBOY! duo this month with *In a Cowboy's Embrace*. Join the fun as Tasha Reynolds falls asleep in the wrong bed and wakes with Cliff Swain, the very *right* cowboy!

This May, flowers aren't the only things blossoming— we've got two very special mothers-to-be! When estranged lovers share one last night of passion, they soon learn they'll never forget *That Night We Made Baby*, Mary Anne Wilson's heartwarming addition to our WITH CHILD... promotion. And as Emily Kingston discovers in Elizabeth Sinclair's charming tale, *The Pregnancy Clause*, where there's a will, there's a baby on the way!

There's something fascinating about a sexy, charismatic man who seems to have it all, and Ingrid Weaver's hero in *Big-City Bachelor* is no exception. Alexander Whitmore has two wonderful children, money, a successful company.... What could he possibly be missing...?

With Harlequin American Romance, you'll always know the exhilarating feeling of falling in love.

Happy reading!

Melissa Jeglinski
Associate Senior Editor

# That Night We Made Baby

## MARY ANNE WILSON

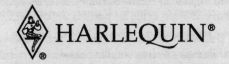

**HARLEQUIN®**

TORONTO • NEW YORK • LONDON
AMSTERDAM • PARIS • SYDNEY • HAMBURG
STOCKHOLM • ATHENS • TOKYO • MILAN • MADRID
PRAGUE • WARSAW • BUDAPEST • AUCKLAND

ISBN 0-373-16826-8

THAT NIGHT WE MADE BABY

Visit us at www.eHarlequin.com

**Printed in U.S.A.**

# ABOUT THE AUTHOR

Mary Anne Wilson is a Canadian transplanted to Southern California where she lives with her husband, three children and an assortment of animals. She knew she wanted to write romances when she found herself "rewriting" the great stories in Literature, such as *A Tale of Two Cities*, to give them "happy endings." Over a ten-year career, she's published thirty romance novels, had her books on bestseller lists, been nominated for Reviewer's Choice Awards and received a Career Achievement Award in Romantic Suspense. She's looking forward to her next thirty books.

## Books by Mary Anne Wilson

### HARLEQUIN AMERICAN ROMANCE

Dear Reader,

As a mother of three, I have always been struck by the power of babies to change their parents' lives forever. Whether they are planned or a surprise, as tiny and helpless as they are, from the moment they exist, they profoundly alter the world around them.

In *That Night We Made Baby*, Samantha Wells is shocked, then thrilled to find herself pregnant with the child of her ex-husband, a man she will always love but knows she will never see again. Nicholas Viera believes he has the life he wants and needs. He knows where he's going, what he wants, and is certain Samantha is his past, and children will never be a part of his future.

Little do both people know, but the "best-laid plans" of expectant parents are far from "set in stone." What they think they want is no match for the tiny life that is a part of both of them, a life that comes with the ability to change or erase every plan they've made.

So, I invite you to share in the story of Samantha and Nicholas and a very unexpected baby who rearranges the future for all of them in *That Night We Made Baby*.

# Prologue

"Reckless driving, an illegal lane change and failure to obey an officer of the law."

Nicholas Viera had lived thirty-eight years without believing in luck. But that all changed the first moment he saw the pretty traffic-court defendant.

He never went into that part of the county courthouse; he didn't deal with that area of the law. But he'd been so intent on something else that he made a wrong turn, pushed open the wrong door and stepped into the wrong chamber.

On that early-summer day, when he heard those charges being read, he looked up to see the defendant—a slender blond woman with her back to him. And Nick knew that luck was very real.

"Your Honor," the blonde said in a quick,

breathy voice, "I was just in the wrong lane and I tried to move over, then this other car wouldn't get out of my way. I tried to get around it, but I couldn't, then I thought if I turned and cut through the parking lot, I'd be able to pull ahead of that car, get in the right lane and go where I was trying to go all along."

From his position at the chamber door, Nick was struck by the earnestness in the woman's voice and by a riot of shoulder-length, sun-bleached blond curls. As he took a step forward, his eyes skimmed over beige slacks that clung to the gentle swell of her hips and showed off incredibly long legs. A clingy white blouse defined slender shoulders that shrugged repeatedly while the woman spoke. Wedge sandals added a couple of inches to her five-foot-five-or-six-inch height, and her hands moved constantly, adding expression to her words.

"I tried, but I didn't realize that the curb cut out like that." Her hands swept out away from her in a grand gesture as her words sped up. "If I had, do you think I would have tried to make that turn? I just never saw it and I thought I could make it, and bam, I hit it."

"Miss Wells, please," the judge said quickly to get a word in edgewise. "According to the officer, you crossed a double yellow line, almost ran into an oncoming car, then hit the curb. When he got there, you wouldn't get out of your vehicle. You were not cooperative. Meanwhile, your car was blocking Wilshire Boulevard at four in the afternoon during rush hour.''

''I told you, I was trying to get into the parking lot and didn't see the curb, then, the tire hit it and just blew up. I thought I might still be able to drive it, but the officer was yelling at me and I got confused.''

Nick found himself smiling as he made his way past the rows of wooden chairs toward the front of the room. He wanted a better look at the woman who wasn't giving up despite the fact that she'd obviously wreaked havoc on the city of Los Angeles with her driving.

''But you were driving the car,'' the judge pointed out with admirable patience. ''You blew the tire, and it's your responsibility.''

''Well, sure, of course, but if the other driver had let me over, I wouldn't have had to do any of those things and the traffic wouldn't have been stopped like that. And the policeman just yelled and yelled.''

''Yes, I guess he would,'' the judge murmured. ''But you could have gone around the block.''

Nick moved closer to the bailiff, and when he finally saw the profile of the formidable Miss Wells, he realized why the judge was being so indulgent with her, or at least why he wasn't simply throwing her in jail and tossing away the key.

The woman was dead serious and absolutely beautiful—seductively appealing with a tiny nose, her chin elevated just a bit with challenge to show the beguiling sweep of her throat. He couldn't help noticing the way the material of her blouse clung to high breasts that strained against the fine fabric with each breath she took. The only sign of nervousness was the way she started fiddling with a locket she wore around her neck.

He'd been so intent on looking at her that he'd almost stopped listening to her. Gradually, her voice filtered in again—a husky, earnest voice. "I had this really important appointment and I was already going to be late and I just had to get there."

"Did you make your appointment?"

She shook her head, making her curls dance softly on her shoulders. "No, Your Honor. I didn't."

He sat back and looked down at her. "That's a shame. Now, are you ready to enter your plea or are you going to want a jury trial?"

"Do I have to have a lawyer for a jury trial?" she asked.

"No, you don't have to have an attorney, but if

I were you and this was my record, I'd consider it."

Nick wasn't looking for more work and he never went into any court thinking about getting a client. Besides, his specialty was criminal law. This woman was just a crazy driver who was far too sexy for her own good. Despite all of that, he saw the way she hesitated, her hand stilling on the locket at her throat, and he found himself stepping in where he knew he probably shouldn't.

"Your Honor, may I approach?"

At that moment, Miss Wells turned, and Nick finally got a good look at her face. She was maybe twenty-five or so, wearing little or no makeup, her incredibly green eyes shadowed by improbably long, dark lashes. There was a faint sprinkling of freckles across her nose. Her pale pink mouth was softly parted in surprise.

"Excuse me, sir?" the judge was saying.

"Nicholas Viera," he said, taking a card out of his pocket and approaching the bench to lay it in front of the judge. "I was wondering if I might be of some help to…" He glanced back at the woman. "Miss Wells."

"I don't understand," the woman said, obviously confused.

"Mr. Viera is apparently an attorney," the judge said as he glanced at the business card.

"And I'm offering to represent the defendant on charges of reckless driving, an illegal lane change and failure to obey an officer of the law." Being improbably desirable certainly wasn't a criminal offense, but if it had been, as good as he was at what he did, he knew he'd never be able to get her off. "And anything else you allege that she did."

"I told the judge that I was just trying to—"

Nick held up a hand to quiet her before she started off on another rambling explanation. "We'll talk," he said, then looked at the judge. "Can we reschedule?"

"If Miss Wells wishes to have counsel, we can put this on the calendar for..." He glanced at his clerk. "How does it look, Rhonda?"

A middle-aged woman at a low desk checked something in front of her, then looked at the judge. "A week today, Your Honor. Ten o'clock."

He looked back at Nick. "How about that?"

Nick looked at Miss Wells. "Is that okay with you?"

Color was creeping into her cheeks, either from embarrassment or self-consciousness or possibly even anger at his high-handed behavior. But she was obviously as intelligent as she was a poor driver. She just nodded and said, "Fine."

The judge said, "See you then, Miss Wells."

"Thank you, Your Honor," Nick said.

The judge reached for another file and looked over at his clerk. "What's next, Rhonda?" he asked, dismissing Nick and his new client.

Nick headed out of the courtroom, and she followed him. When he paused to open the door, he stood aside to let her step out into the corridor. The air stirred as she went by, touched by a hint of freshness mingling with her delicate floral scent. Then she stopped and turned to look at him as he let the door swing shut behind him.

Nick stared into those green eyes, and although his world wasn't given to flights of fantasy he could feel his world start to shake. The impact of her gaze almost made him flinch. The strength of his attraction to her was beyond anything he'd felt before. An unsettling experience for him and an intriguing one.

She brushed at her hair, exposing a palm stained with green paint, then her tongue touched her full bottom lip. The action stirred something in him, and he realized that this woman had made him want her before he even knew her first name.

SAMANTHA WELLS NEVER EVEN knew there was a Nicholas Viera in the world until the striking man in a well-tailored gray suit had suddenly spoken and started toward the bench. Frustration and fear about the possibility of losing her driver's license had been making her slightly crazy at that moment. Then he was there, a man who filled the whole room with his presence, who moved as if he owned the world. Nicholas Viera.

The moment she met the intensity of his gaze, everything had started to blur, to run together in a rush of reactions. Sexy, definitely very male, and disturbing. But also so controlled and at ease in his surroundings that she envied him. She'd tried to concentrate, to figure out what he was doing there, and then he'd said something about representing her.

She didn't understand at first and the only thing she could think of was the fact that his mouth was wide and hinted at a hidden smile. And that his eyes were neither green nor brown, but a rich hazel color that was set off by tanned skin and dark brown hair flecked with gray.

She'd felt herself flush when he turned those intense eyes on her again, asking her if that was okay with her. She'd realized that the judge had been rescheduling her court date—as if she could afford to have this man come back with her in a week. She knew how far-fetched that was, but she'd just nodded and said softly, "Fine."

Now she was standing in the courthouse corridor with Nicholas Viera. He held out a business card to her.

"'Viera, Combs and O'Neill. Nicholas Viera,'" she read, along with an office address in Bel Air. An elegantly simple, obviously expensive card, done in heavy ivory stock, it had probably cost more to print them up than she had in her bank account all last year.

She studied the owner of the card, a six-foot-tall man in a suit that defined his whipcord-lean build. An expensive suit. She looked up into his face, at features that were as untraditionally handsome as they were attractive. He had a strong, clean-shaven jaw, dark brows and a nose that was slightly crooked. It all came together with the rest of the man to make a disturbingly sexy package.

Very upscale, probably all Ivy League. And no matter how attracted she was to him, he was totally out of the league of a struggling artist who could barely pay for her share of an apartment she occupied with three other young women. "Thanks for getting me out of there," she said. "Have a nice day."

"What?"

"Thanks. I appreciate what you did in there. Now I've got time to figure out what to do." She lifted the card. "Do you want it back, Mr. Viera?"

"No, keep it," he said. "Call me Nick, and your name is…?"

"Samantha Wells."

"Miss Wells."

"Sam, please."

"You looked as if you needed a little help in there."

She barely contained a smile at the observation. "A little help? I could use a whole law firm right about now, but I can't even afford a paralegal, let alone a real, honest-to-goodness lawyer." She pushed his card into her purse, then held out her hand to him as she prepared to break whatever connection was forming between herself and this man. "But thanks again."

He took her hand in his, and she was very aware of how large and strong his hand was. It surprised her when he didn't shake her hand but turned it over, palm up. Then he looked at her and that hint of a smile became a reality, an explosive reality for her. "So it's not just crazy driving you're here for, is it?"

"What?" she asked, her voice verging on breathless. "Of course it is. I mean, I'm not crazy, but it's this ticket thing and—"

The smile deepened. "Shhh, let me figure this out. I get paid big bucks to be insightful about my clients. Between you and me, I figure that you're in here for counterfeiting, but you're having trouble with the ink."

She felt heat rush into her face again and cursed

the fact that she blushed so easily. She was always a bit self-conscious about her hands and the stains that never seemed to come out. How could she feel as if this man's presence totally surrounded her? Or that she'd missed him all her life, yet had never known he existed until right then?

"Green. The color of money," he said, and traced the faint stain on her palm with his forefinger. "Not regulation green, but close."

She drew back, closing her hand into a fist behind her back. "That particular green is the color of the trees in the mist on an island in Puget Sound, and I worked hard to create it before I had to come to court."

"Oh, you're a housepainter?"

That smile was there again, and she could feel herself being seduced by a simple expression. It had never happened to her before with any man. Men who were a blur to her now, men who hadn't been important enough in her life to even remember now. "No, an artist, or at least I'm trying to be. You know, landscapes, seascapes, portraits? That's why I was in such a hurry when I…I had my problem with the car. I was seeing a gallery owner about a showing and I didn't want to be late." She grimaced at the memory of her call to the owner and finding out he was gone and wouldn't be back for two weeks. "I was too late."

"I know some art gallery owners. What's your medium—black velvet?"

That made her laugh out loud, and she had to cover her mouth with her hand to control the sound that echoed in the corridor. The next thing she knew, Nick was touching her hand, easing it down, but not letting her go. She felt his fingers close around hers and she didn't fight the contact, not when it seemed to be anchoring her in some way. "I...I'm sorry," she said, suddenly having trouble taking her next breath.

"Don't be. Let's go where we can laugh," he said.

"Mr. Viera, listen to me. I'm broke. I'm the proverbial struggling artist, and if I get an attorney, it's going to have to be a public defender, but I thank you for everything you've done."

He leaned a bit closer to her. "Did I mention money?"

She was confused again. She didn't know what to deal with first—his offering to help her or that sensation of his being her anchor. "I assumed—"

"Never assume anything with an attorney," he said with a half smile. "This is called pro bono work. Free. A way for an attorney to atone for those clients he wishes he'd never represented, but clients who pay the big bucks. To be honest with you, I'm good. Unless you're a serial killer, I can get you off.'' Another smile played on his lips. ''And even if you are a serial killer, I can probably get you off for that, too. Now, can we go someplace and talk about this?''

He was a stranger, yet Sam knew she was going to go with him. She knew that he could help her and she knew something else. Whatever was happening to her at that moment, Nicholas Viera was going to change her life.

# Chapter One

Nick was sicker than he could ever remember being since he was a kid at boarding school. He'd canceled his last appointment for the day, gone home, taken medication the doctor had given him, then crawled into bed just after seven. In his house overlooking the ocean, he'd sunk rapidly into sleep that, at first, had been peaceful and a break from the aches and pains caused by the flu.

But sometime during the night, that all changed. A dream came, a dream about Sam and him. There had been dreams since she'd left, vague, unformed dreams that left him frustrated and restless the next day. But he wasn't prepared for this dream. Maybe it came from the medication, but whatever it was, the dream was vivid and clear.

Sam had exploded into his life months ago, tipping his world with her presence. Then she was gone and he'd tried to forget her and go on with his life. But at that moment, her image was burned into his mind and soul. It was so clear he wondered if the dream was reality and his life was the dream.

Sam with the golden curls, slender beauty, those green eyes. The vision was so real his whole being ached. The fascination and attraction he'd experienced from his first glimpse of her in the courtroom were still there—a basic, disturbing reality in the dream. He could see himself going to her, wild need filling him, surrounding him, threatening to smother him.

The dream was filled with a hunger that had a life of its own. He saw himself reach out for her, his hands touching silky skin. He could feel heat consume his world that had been filled with only coldness until then—a coldness that reappeared when she'd left him.

He felt the heaviness of her breasts in his hands, her hips pressing against his hardness. When his lips covered hers, he felt himself melting into her. He became so infused with her that there was no division between them. Just one person. One need. One hunger.

In a single jarring moment, all that dissolved. She was ripped away from him and Nick's only reality was solitude. There was no contact, no heat, no satisfaction, no losing himself. Then he realized a phone was ringing.

He woke with a sickening jolt. His ragged breathing was punctuated by the ringing of the phone. The sheets tangled around his naked body, he pushed himself upright in the mussed bed. The room was bathed in the cold light of morning, and a sudden sense of loss all but choked him. Emptiness echoed around him and his skin was filmed with moisture.

The phone on the nightstand rang again, and with one swipe at his damp face, he reached for the receiver.

His hand shook as it closed over the cold plastic, and he passed the unsteadiness off as part of his illness and the medication he was taking. That's why he had such a dream. God knew what the combination of being sick and taking medication could do to a man's mind, let alone his body. Crazy, insane visions of the past were banished. He never dwelled on mistakes in his life and he didn't intend to start now.

Nick pressed the phone to his ear, closed his eyes to the view of the ocean visible through the French doors and started to speak. But he stopped when he realized it was his voice mail ringing with his messages. He'd put a hold on all calls last night, hoping that whatever illness he had would be gone by morning. But he wasn't that lucky. Then he heard the machine's voice saying that the message had been left just about the time he'd gone to bed last night.

His attorney started to speak and Nick silently cursed the quirks of timing that fate seemed to possess. The call was about Samantha.

"Nick, it's Jerod Danforth. I'd hoped to catch you home. The papers are ready. Come by the office at your convenience to sign them. Then the divorce is final. A few minutes, that's all. A simple procedure. Call me about it. Oh, by the way, congratulations on getting Griffith off. Very nice indeed. Almost makes me wish I was in trouble with the law to see you do your stuff in court. See you soon."

Nick dropped the receiver back down with a clatter and sank against the smooth coolness of the bleached wood headboard. Damn it. He didn't need this. The last thing he wanted to deal with right now was a marriage that had had about as much substance as a flash of lightning. It had been intense and blinding for a heartbeat before it had faded away forever.

"A simple procedure," Danforth had said.

Nothing had been simple with Sam. Not from his first meeting with her, to the moment when she'd walked out of his world six months ago. He'd go by Danforth's offices as soon as he could and finally put the madness Sam had brought into his life to rest. Shifting, he could still feel the tight, uncomfortable aching in his body.

Yes, he needed to put this all to rest and forget it ever happened. Then he got out of bed and headed to the bathroom and a cool shower.

SAM WAS JUST ON HER WAY out of her Brentwood hotel room when the phone rang. Hurrying back to the phone by the bed, she picked up the receiver and said, "Yes, hello?"

"Samantha, it's May Douglas."

Sam was surprised to hear from her landlady. The elderly widow lived in an old Victorian house on several acres overlooking the ocean in Jensen Pass, a small town in northern California. The cottage where Sam lived and worked had been built for May's husband, a writer, and Sam—when she was a child—had often thought it looked enchanted. So far it had been a place of healing and a place of safety.

She'd gone to Jensen Pass when she left Nick and found the cottage was available for rent. It had been perfect. The isolation and the peace to be found there were just perfect. Even Mrs. Douglas was perfect. A quiet, interesting lady, she liked roses and afternoon teas. A grandmotherly sort whom Sam had come to like very much.

"Mrs. Douglas, how wonderful to hear your voice," Sam said. "There isn't anything wrong, is there?"

"Oh, no, dear, nothing's wrong. Owen is doing better, but he's a bit put out because I've had to give him medicine that he hates. He just won't take it nicely. But then again, Owen is so sensitive and opinionated."

The lady surely hadn't called to tell Sam about the well-being of Owen or his medicinal regime. "Yes, he certainly is," Sam said.

"Oh, did you get the showing?"

"The gallery owner is very interested and seems to think the show could do well. I have to ship more pieces down and he'll make a decision then."

"He'll love them, dear. Are you coming back tomorrow?"

"Yes, I plan to. In the afternoon."

"Wonderful. Tea and conversation, the two things I've missed so much until you rented the cottage."

Mrs. Douglas was tiny and spry with silver hair and the propensity for anything lavender, even in her gardens that hugged the top of the cliff over-looking the beach. "Yes, I'll look forward to that.'' She was about to say goodbye when Mrs. Douglas spoke again.

''Oh, my, I almost forgot why I called. I was at the cottage watering your plants, and the phone rang. I know it could have gone to your machine, but that's so impersonal, so I hope it's okay that I took the call?''

''Of course it is. Was it important?''

''Just a minute,'' she said, then Sam heard the rustle of paper before Mrs. Douglas spoke again. ''Let me see if I can read my own handwriting here. Yes, it was a Mr. Danforth's secretary calling to let you know that the final divorce papers are ready for your signature and he wants you to contact him at your earliest convenience.''

Sam sank onto the bed, her legs suddenly unsteady. The divorce. Why had she thought she could come to Los Angeles without being touched by Nick in one way or another? ''Anything else?''

''No, not really. Except you told me you were only married for three months. I would have thought you could just have gotten an annulment instead of a divorce. I mean, after three months, that's hardly a marriage.''

The elderly lady was more right than she knew about her marriage hardly being a marriage. ''Nick took care of it, and I told him to do whatever he needed. He's an attorney, so I assumed he'd know how best to handle the situation.''

Sam closed her eyes but opened them immediately when a vision of Nick popped into her head. Damn it, she'd been trying to put him behind her for six months. She'd changed her life by putting almost the entire state of California between them and rebuilding her own life. But suddenly he was there, tall and lean, his face a mix of planes and angles, eyes so intense she'd been sure he could see into her soul.

One of the many things she'd been wrong about with Nick was that he hadn't been able to see into her soul. He'd never even known her. He'd wanted to be with her but had never wanted the marriage she'd finally insisted on. Just a few of the many things she'd found out about too late. She shook her head and banished the thoughts and memories.

''There's no point in looking back,'' she said. Especially not when all that did was stir up a sense of loss and frustration and pain. A sense of being so wrong.

''You're right, Samantha. The future is where your life is going. You're young and have your whole life ahead of you. And you know, dear, you can never go back.''

She wouldn't want to. ''Thanks for the message, Mrs. Douglas. I'll see you tomorrow.''

"Have a safe trip, dear, and come by the house to let me know when you're home."

"Yes, I will," she said, and hung up.

The divorce was a formality. A legality. Nothing more. But that logic couldn't shut out memories of that horrible conversation she'd overheard the night her marriage had ended. Nick and his partner and friend, Greg O'Neill, had been out on the deck of the house in Malibu, drinking in the darkness. She'd heard their loud conversation all the way from the living room.

"My God, Greg," she'd heard Nick say, "I've gotten myself in a real mess. This marriage..." She'd heard the clink of glass on glass and looked through the doorway out to the deck. She'd barely been able to make Nick out as he stood with his back to the house, staring at the ocean. "I don't even know how it happened," he'd said to Greg. "I'd only known her two weeks." She tried to stop the memory but it kept going.

"You bribed a judge, didn't you?" Greg had replied with a burst of laughter. She'd stopped a few feet from the door and waited for Nick to join in, to make it all a joke.

But that hadn't happened. "'Bribe' isn't the word, but he owed me a favor. If I'd had to wait three days, who knows?"

"You wouldn't have done it?" Greg had asked.

"I would have come to my senses," he'd said after a long, painful pause. That had been the truth. She'd heard it in his voice. There was a blur of hurtful words, then Nick saying, "Marriage isn't a normal state. Who ever thought up this concept of 'forever' with one person?"

Sam had known things were bad between them, that they were strangers in so many ways. As much as she'd craved a family, a connection that she'd never had from her life growing up in foster homes, she'd known at that moment that happily-ever-after was never going to happen with Nick.

Pain and sorrow had filled her and she'd known what she had to do then. As she knew what she had to do now. Once she signed the divorce papers, she could go back to her real life and start forgetting Nick...again.

## Chapter Two

Late that afternoon, when Nick got to Danforth's plush offices he was beyond sick. He had aches where he'd never felt aches before, and there was an unwelcome sense of his world not being right. He had to make a conscious effort to walk into the beige-on-beige reception area and get the day over with.

A simple nod to the receptionist who sat behind an intricate marble desk cost him dearly when a throbbing headache materialized behind his eyes. He grimaced. "Marge. I just need a minute of his time," he said.

"I'm not sure he's free to—"

"I won't take a minute," he said as he kept going, unnerved by a wave of weakness that washed over him.

God, he hated weakness of all kinds, especially in himself. He dealt with it all too often with his clients, and the only concession he'd made to being sick today was to take his medication.

But the medicine was hardly helping at all. And it hadn't helped earlier when he'd had three cases on the docket and had to deal with one client who had been a no-show at a bail hearing. And he'd been trying to figure out for the past hour why a case he should have been able to plea-bargain had gone to trial. Now he had to sign the divorce papers.

He rapped on the door and flinched slightly from the headache that had just kicked up a notch and from Danforth's booming greeting as the man opened the door. Danforth looked a little surprised to see him.

"Wasn't expecting you," he said in a baritone that served the man well in court but seemed brutally loud at that moment. "You never called back so I didn't know if you'd picked up the message." He moved back a bit. "But come on in."

"I got your message first thing this morning," Nick muttered as he entered the office. "So I came by after—"

His words stopped dead as the dream from the night before materialized not more than ten feet from him. A couple of long strides and he could have touched Sam, a Sam in a clinging blue sundress. Her blond curls had been all but banished by a short wedge cut that made her face all the more delicate-looking and her eyes all the more green.

A dream? A hallucination induced by the medication? He instinctively took a step forward but stopped as the image took one sharp breath and whispered his name.

"Nicholas."

He heard it, really heard it, a voice that he'd almost forgotten existed until that moment. A voice that belonged to the only person he didn't want to see right then. This was no dream, no illusion or hallucination, but reality. Samantha was real, so painfully real that he longed for the dream. Something he could vanquish simply by waking up.

He regrouped, more shaken then he could comprehend, and gasped for control. He took a breath of his own, then was able to speak in a remarkably normal voice. "Sam. I had no idea you were in Los Angeles."

"I...I'm just in town for a few days. I'm going back tomorrow."

He tried to remember where Danforth had said she'd gone, what her mailing address had been. Jensen Pass. That was it—a tiny coastal village north of San Francisco. That's where she was supposed to be, not standing motionless by a massive cherry desk, with papers in her hands, staring at him as if he were an alien life-form. She was making him feel even more disoriented than he had been.

As Sam stood a bit straighter, Danforth spoke quickly. "This situation might be rather awkward for the two of you," he said. "Tell you what, Nick. I can have the papers messengered over to your office tomorrow."

Nick needed air, but he didn't leave. Instead, he pushed aside everything that seemed to be bombarding him and took control. He wasn't about to have this hanging over his head for one more day. "No reason to put it off," Nick said. "Let's get it over with."

The words came out with an edge he hadn't intended, and he didn't miss the way Sam's expression tightened. Or the fact that he had to narrow his eyes to dull the sharp vividness of her being. But narrowed eyes couldn't stop the unsteadiness that persisted inside him or the way his head continued pounding.

"Actually, I was ready to leave," Sam said, and her lashes lowered just enough to shadow her eyes and guard her emotions. She was putting the papers in a large envelope, talking as she slid them inside, her voice in some way filtering into his consciousness. "I'm finished here. I just came..." She ex-

haled, and the sound echoed through Nick. Not that
there was an echo in the luxurious office. The echo
was inside him, another extra from being sick that
he didn't welcome. Her gaze went to Danforth.
"I'll read them, then get them back to you as soon
as I can."

"I can send a messenger to your hotel for them
if you just call the office when they're ready."

"I won't be there. I'm leaving first thing tomorrow, so I'll get them back to you."

"You've got Express Mail in—what's it called,
Jensen Pass?" Nick asked with no idea why he
would say something that sounded so sarcastic.

She turned to him, holding the envelope in one
hand, her other hand nervously twisting her locket.
The locket had been her mother's and at one time
had held a picture of him. "Ever the logical
mind," she said, bitterness edging her words.
"Rest assured we have all the amenities in Jensen
Pass. Electricity, running water, indoor plumbing
and Express Mail. We're not exactly in the boon-
docks there."

He had no idea what Jensen Pass was or wasn't,
but he did know that for some reason his sarcasm
was growing. "You left all those luxuries behind
to come here to get the papers?"

She glanced down at the envelope in her hand

as if she'd all but forgotten about it. "Oh, no, I had no idea…"

Her tongue touched her pale lips, and the sight sent a jolt through him that he found himself clearing his throat to control. God, what was so wrong with him that he could literally taste her in his mouth?

"I was in the city to see about a showing. This whole paper-signing thing…it's just a…" She nibbled on her bottom lip and he filled in the word for her.

"A bonus?"

Her expression tightened again, this time drawing a fine line between her eyes and compressing her mouth. Color touched her cheeks. "Not hardly," she said as her chin lifted just a bit. "But it is convenient."

Suddenly, his legs felt rubbery and he moved farther into the room. Veering away from Sam, he reached for the closest chair and gripped the high leather back with one hand. Danforth was talking, and Nick had to force himself to focus on the lawyer to comprehend what he was saying.

"Actually, Samantha's right. It is convenient. You're both here, so we can get this over with right now."

Nick actually needed the support of the chair, and if he hadn't been so distracted by Sam's unexpected appearance, that would have really annoyed him. "Sure, whatever," Nick muttered.

"I don't want anything from Nick," Sam stated, "so it should be very simple. I just don't see why we couldn't have gotten an annulment."

Danforth looked at Nick. "You never mentioned that."

"I never thought of it," he murmured, his hand tightening on the leather chair. "But if Sam wants to do that instead of—"

"Well, you'd need proof of fraud to get an annulment since I assume the marriage was consummated."

"No, no," Sam said quickly. "This is almost finished. That would be foolish."

Nick saw the color in Sam's cheeks rise even more, and she was staring hard at the envelope in her hand. Fraud? How about stupidity? And the marriage had been consummated—over and over again. Sex had been just about the only thing between them that they had both wanted—except for this divorce.

He felt a treacherous response to the memories as they started to return, and he moved carefully to sink into the chair.

"A divorce is fine," Sam was saying, holding on to the envelope with her left hand, a hand without a ring. The single diamond was where she'd left it—in the side drawer of his desk. He hadn't looked at it since she'd walked out. "But I need to read the papers before I sign," she continued.

"Of course," Danforth said.

Sam let go of the locket and skimmed her hand behind her neck, lifting her chin slightly and exposing her throat for a flashing instant. Nick was suddenly bombarded with the memory of the feel of her skin against his, that heat and silk, the pleasure that came in waves, the sensation of her pulse against his lips. He cleared his throat abruptly, tightening his hands on the arms of the chair and forcing himself to make small talk. "How's your work going?"

Her green-eyed gaze turned to him, and the impact made his head swim. "Fine. I'm working on several paintings, actually. They might be picked up for the Orleans series." He must have looked blank because she went on to explain. "It's a children's series of morality books."

"Morality books," he repeated.

"Honor, truth, loyalty...doing the right thing."

He had the strangest idea that she was rebuking him somehow. "It's a series?"

"Five titles in the planning. They saw some other children's illustrations I did and they liked them." She shrugged slightly. "They liked them very much."

For a moment, he thought she was going to smile and he found himself bracing for the impact. He remembered her smiles, and he remembered what her smile had done to him when he first met her. He remembered and wished he hadn't.

"Obviously, you're good," he murmured. "It sounds as if you're doing well."

Looking up at her now, he found himself confused about why he'd let this woman walk out on him. He tried to focus, to grab at a reason, then it came to him in a wrenching thud when she spoke again.

"I am. I love working on things for children."

Children. At least he remembered one of the many reasons why their marriage had dissolved. They'd been on the beach at dawn, watching the sun rise, and she'd hugged her legs, staring out at the water.

"What a place for kids to grow up."

He'd made some noncommittal answer like "Yeah, great," but he'd been paying more attention to her tiny blue bikini and wondering how soon they could get back to the house so he could make love to her.

"I've always wanted to raise my kids by the ocean. That was the best time of my life, up in Jensen Pass. The ocean was like freedom to me, and I always knew that when I got married, I'd be by the ocean, and my kids would swim like fish.''

He'd been tracing her jawline with the tip of his finger but stopped. ''That's a nice fantasy,'' he'd murmured, hoping he could banish the whole idea that easily.

But nothing about Sam had been easy. ''It's what I want. What I've always dreamed of. A husband and children. All the trimmings.''

He couldn't pass that off as another rough spot in a rushed marriage. They were two people who had met and married in two weeks, two strangers who had desperately tried to reach out to each other. He hid from her words, from a dream life that he didn't want. All he wanted was her.

He didn't want children. He didn't want to be tied down. But he wanted her. He'd stood, lifted her into his arms and carried her to the house. Their lovemaking that time had been explosive, and it had also been the last time he'd touched her.

Their relationship had been too intense and all-consuming. All he'd known while they were together was that nothing else mattered. Not when she smiled. Not when she touched him. At least, not at first while they were lost in each other's arms.

''Children. Good.'' He spoke past an odd tightness in his throat. ''I'm glad things are working out for you.'' He looked away, the thought of that last day bringing bitterness in a rush. He'd been wrong, so wrong. His mistake. His impulsiveness. His decision. A marriage that should have never been. She'd needed the commitment of marriage, and he'd gone along with it, never thinking about the consequences of two people finally looking at each other and finding out they were strangers. Husband and wife, but strangers.

''How have you been doing?'' Sam asked abruptly.

He looked back at her, bracing himself this time, expecting that rush of need and desire that came no matter how rationally he tried to fight it when he was near her. ''Working. I keep busy.''

''Of course, I remember,'' she said softly. ''Still fighting for the bad guy? Giving a defense to those with no defense?''

His headache increased as echoes from the past bombarded him. ''How can you defend me when you know darn well that I did all that stuff the judge read to you? I mean, I didn't intend to do it, but I'm guilty.''

His response now came as easily as the same response had come so long ago. ''Everyone deserves a defense and I'm good at it.'' He'd gotten her off with a fine, driving school and a restricted license for three months. A slap on the wrist after everything she'd done. "I got *you* off, didn't I?"

"Yes, you did," she said, and his headache grew when her chin lifted just a fraction of an inch. "But then again, I wasn't a serial killer."

"You drove like one," he said.

Sam felt her face burn, and she was furious that she was still so vulnerable to everything Nick said or did. It had to be the shock. When she'd come to Los Angeles, she'd known she wouldn't be going anywhere near Malibu and she certainly hadn't expected to see him walk through the door. Not any more than she'd expected that the sight of him would rock the world under her feet.

She turned from him and the way he seemed to fill all the space in the room, the way he'd always filled the space around her. She concentrated on the attorney behind the desk. But nothing she did could stop her from feeling Nick's presence beside her. She didn't have to inhale to know that he was so close she almost felt the air stir as he shifted in the leather chair.

She didn't have to turn to be assailed by his image, an image burned into her mind. The navy suit, the pin-striped shirt with a deep red tie. His hair, a bit longer than it once had been, swept back from a hard face. Angles and planes. Those eyes. The one constant with Nick was that he was as sexy as hell. Even when he looked as if he wasn't feeling well.

She couldn't block out the image even when she wasn't looking at him. He still had the same effect on her as he had the first moment they'd met, the first time he spoke to her in that low, rough voice, the first moment he touched her. She took a deep breath and knew she needed to go home, but she couldn't till tomorrow morning. Until then, she just needed to be out of this office and to put Nick behind her.

"Mr. Danforth, I tell you what. I'll get these back to you before I fly out tomorrow," she told the attorney.

"That's fine." The man frowned at the two of them, probably glad that she was leaving and any explosion wouldn't happen. "Just fine."

She picked up her small white purse, then turned and walked away. The door was close enough for her to reach out and touch when she heard Nick's voice call out, "Sam?"

She stopped but didn't turn around. She didn't need to look at Nick, the man she married, the man whose touch could make all reason flee, the man who could make her ache with just the sound of his voice. She held the doorknob so tightly her hand ached. All she wanted to do was cross the room and make some contact with him. "Yes?"

"I'm sorry."

Sam stood very still, his words hanging between them, and she didn't know what to do. He was sorry. For some reason, that centered her. It killed whatever had been happening, whatever craziness was growing inside her, and in its place came a startling anger. She remembered. That moment she knew she'd have to leave. That moment she realized that Nick was a stranger.

Nick and Greg O'Neill on the deck of the Malibu house. She'd been gone, losing herself in her painting. The morning had started badly with a sense of something wrong, but she hadn't been able to figure it out. There had been so many rough spots in the short marriage, but that morning, something had changed.

When they'd come back to the house from the beach, their lovemaking had been incredible and almost desperate. Now she realized she had sensed their relationship was over. That was the last time they'd made love. She'd immersed herself in her painting all day, then when night came, she'd heard voices in some other part of the house.

Wiping her hands on a rag, she'd gone toward the voices but stopped when she realized that Nick and Greg O'Neill were talking on the deck overlooking the beach. There were no lights on, just a partial moon, and the sound of Nick's voice seemed to be everywhere in the air.

"My God, Greg, I've gotten myself in a real mess. This marriage…I don't even know how it happened, and now Sam's talking about kids. Next thing you know, she'll be wanting a picket fence and daisies."

Greg had laughed, saying something about bribing a judge and favors owed.

She'd waited for Nick to laugh and make it all into a joke. But he never had. Instead he spoke about marriage as if it were a disease. His voice was low, slightly slurred from drinking and filled with remorse. "It's my fault, and if I could undo it, I would in an instant."

"You wouldn't even have wanted to meet Sam?" Greg had asked.

"Oh, hell, meet her? Yes. I wanted her from the first minute I saw her in that courtroom, green all over her hands, telling the judge that she was just trying to get to where she was going and didn't understand why everyone was so upset with her driving." There was a pause, then he laughed, but the sound was almost ugly. "Too bad it couldn't have just been different."

She had tried so hard to block his words, but they never went away. "Like what, an affair?" Greg had asked.

"Absolutely. That would have been perfect. But marriage? Marriage isn't a normal state. Who ever thought up this concept of 'forever' with one person?"

"You don't love her?"

She'd held her breath until Nick spoke again. "Love? I want her. I can't stop that. But love? There's no such thing."

During their short marriage, he had never once said he loved her. They were strangers in so many ways. But she hadn't known about the regret on Nick's part. She'd believed that he loved her even if he couldn't say it. She'd deluded herself. That tore at her more than anything, and in that moment in the dark, she'd seen clearly what she had to do.

The dreams that had kept her going through a lifetime alone were shattered. Her dreams of meeting a man, falling madly in love, being loved in return and having his children, died that night.

Her last act was to ask Nick one simple question, and even before he spoke, she knew it was over. So she gave him what he wanted—an out. And he'd taken it.

She bit her lips hard, the past hammering against her, and she would have left Danforth's offices right then if Nick hadn't spoken again.

"Sam? I said I was sorry."

She took a breath, trying to steady the way her

heart was bouncing in her chest, then made herself look back at him over her shoulder. He was still sitting in the chair, his eyes narrowed, his hands pressed to his thighs. She was sorry, too. So very sorry at that moment. And it made her ache even more. She was sorry for ever cuddling against him in the night, for ever touching him or letting him touch her. She was so damned sorry it was pathetic.

That thought was clear and sharp, as painful as anything she'd ever felt. "What are you sorry for?" she asked, her voice tight.

"For not being what you needed."

She exhaled, a slightly shaky action, and spoke the truth. "It's not your fault. The man I thought you were just never showed up," she said quietly. "It was my fault for thinking he would." Then she did leave. She went through the door, closed it and hurried through the reception area, looking neither right nor left.

She went out into the hallway to the elevators and didn't feel as if she could breathe until she'd pushed the down button. Fifty feet and three closed doors were between herself and Nick, and yet she could still almost feel him behind her.

She held the purse and envelope against her chest so tightly that the clasp on her purse was biting into her ribs, but she didn't ease her grip.

For six months she'd had a life without Nick, a life that wasn't what she'd dreamed she'd have, but it had been good at the cottage. It had been calm and peaceful. But just one meeting with him had toppled whatever balance she'd found.

"Mrs. Viera?"

Startled by the sound of a name she hadn't heard in months, she realized that the elevator doors were wide open. She didn't have a clue how long she'd been standing there or why a slightly built, elderly gentleman dressed all in black was in the car watching her with a smile.

## Chapter Three

For a minute Sam thought her mind was playing tricks on her, that she'd imagined hearing her married name. Until she stepped into the car and the small man asked, "You are Mrs. Viera, aren't you?"

She didn't recognize him. "I'm sorry. Do I know you?"

"Simon Curtis," he murmured. "We met at a gathering at Judge Wagner's place last July fourth?"

She remembered fireworks and music and a lot of people. Nick knew so many people. He drew them like a magnet, just the way he had drawn her at first. "Oh, of course," she said, being polite and not because she remembered him. "How are you?"

"Just checking in on an associate. How are you?"

"Fine." She lied.

"And your painting, how is that going?"

"Fine, thank you," she said, thankful to get her mind on better things. "I might be having a show at the Berry Gallery."

"Oh, my, that's very impressive. I was there for a show last year, and, my dear, it's a wonderful place to display your work."

"Oh, I know. It's not set yet, but they're very interested."

"Your husband must be very proud of you." He smiled at her. "I could tell when you were together at the party that you two were special together. I'm just so pleased that it's all working out so nicely."

His words were like a blow to her.

She stared at the flash of floor numbers as the elevator descended. "We're divorcing," she said bluntly, just to get out the words she'd said before, words that now sounded incredibly horrible in the confines of the elevator.

"Oh, I'm sorry. I just thought… I really am very sorry."

"You couldn't have known," she murmured.

The elevator stopped at the second floor and Mr. Curtis hesitated as the doors opened. His clear blue eyes looked sad. "My dear, it was lovely seeing you again. I do hope that you have great success with your art, and that you find what you're looking for."

Her fingers crushed the envelope that held her

divorce papers. "Thank you," she said, not at all sure what she was looking for anymore.

He bowed, an old-fashioned gesture, then turned and stepped out. The doors closed and Sam was alone, very alone. She hadn't cried much since leaving Nick, having known that she'd made a mistake and had to go on with her life alone, like always. But right then her eyes burned and she swiped a hand over her face.

When the elevator opened to the parking area, she headed for her rental car. As she neared the small blue vehicle, she realized that she was shaking.

She got into the car, tossed the envelope and her purse onto the passenger seat, then closed the door. Inserting the key in the ignition, she started the motor, then as easily as it started, it died. She tried again, but this time it coughed, clicked and wouldn't even turn over. Three more tries only met with a cranking sound. And then nothing.

The curse she uttered rattled in the confines of the car. If she had never left Jensen Pass, if she had never agreed to come to Los Angeles to talk to the gallery owner, if Mrs. Douglas hadn't called with the message…. If…if…if…

She jumped when someone rapped sharply on the window. She turned and acknowledged how screwy the day had become when she found herself looking out at Nick.

Nick had stayed in Danforth's office long enough to get a drink of cold water, sign the myriad of papers and tell Danforth that he was going home to go to bed. But when he stepped out of the elevator into the parking garage, he heard the cranking of an engine and stopped by the little blue car to lend a hand. He was surprised to see the driver was Sam.

He motioned for her to roll down the window. "I thought you'd be gone by now."

"So did I," she muttered as she sat back and took one swipe at the steering wheel with the flat of her hand. "The car won't start. Stupid machine."

This was so familiar to him, it was like a warm wave of the past rolling over him, a seductive wave that beckoned to him. Sam in a car that she'd disabled by some means, a perfectly good car until she got in behind the wheel and had her way with it. "Necessary evils?"

Her eyes flashed and she nodded. "I knew I should have just used taxis." She bit her lip. "I thought renting a car would be a good idea. It's dead. It won't start at all."

"This might seem like a dumb question, but do you have gas?"

"I just filled it," she said.

"You've got the gear shift in Park?"

She glanced between the seats, then back at him. "It's right on the 'P', as in Park."

He crouched down by the door, bringing himself to eye level with her as he gripped the window frame with both of his hands to keep his balance. "And the key...?"

"Yes, yes, I have the right key," she muttered.

"Just checking," he said, not about to remind her of the time she'd sat in his Jeep for a good five minutes trying to figure out why the key wouldn't fit in the ignition. He'd finally rescued her by pointing out that the house key wasn't meant to be used for the car. Despite feeling like death warmed over, he could sense a smile forming and tried to hide it. "Sorry, I had to ask."

"It's the car key, not the hotel key. Those plastics cards don't even begin to fit."

Her tension was easing, and there was the echo of a smile at her full lips. God, he hoped against hope that her smile wouldn't find its full expression. He remembered its effect on him from the past, and he didn't need that now.

"Good point," he said softly.

"Besides, all your keys looked alike, and any car you had was so damned complicated." The suggestion of the smile was gone. "I'm just not mechanical."

He'd forgotten how it felt to spar with Sam and tease her. Even his persistent headache didn't kill the pleasure. "Not being mechanical doesn't explain hitting curbs and blowing out tires," he said.

"I did that one time. That's it."

"No arrests for reckless driving lately?"

Sam stared at Nick, the past washing over her. She hated this car, and hated being stuck here, hated the fact that she was so damned aware of Nick's hands gripping the door frame. Strong hands. Hands that had touched her so softly. She exhaled in a rush and muttered, "I wasn't actually arrested, and you know it."

"I made sure you weren't."

"The damned car just won't start." She noticed the paleness that tinged his complexion and the way his hair clung to his temples. "Are you sick?"

"I've felt better."

"Then why don't you just go home? You don't look well, and I need to get ahold of the car rental company."

"I've just got a touch of the flu. Nothing big."

"Well, you look terrible," she said, not about to mention that even sick, the man was striking. Instead, she turned from him, reached for her purse and took out the car rental packet. "There has to be a pay phone around here," she said.

She sensed him shift and when she looked back at him, he was holding out a tiny cell phone to her. "Be my guest." When she hesitated, he shrugged. "No germs, I promise."

She took the phone and punched in the number. When she got in touch with the rental company, they promised to send out a replacement car, but they had a two-hour wait on any service right then. She gave them the address, told them to pick up the car, keep the replacement car and she'd take a taxi. She closed the phone and turned back to Nick. Thankfully, he was standing straight now and back a few feet from the car door.

"Cabs in L.A. are few and far between, and this time of day..." He shook his head slightly. "That's not going to be easy."

She picked up her purse, left the keys in the ignition and got out. "I've found a taxi in this city before," she muttered as she slammed the door shut.

"So, you have," he said.

She faced Nick. In the harsh overhead light, she could see things she hadn't noticed in Danforth's office. The fine lines at his eyes, the faint paleness that was there despite a tan, and the fact that the top button on his shirt was open, the tie gone. He really didn't look well. It bothered her a lot that she felt real concern and maybe a bit of protectiveness toward the man. She didn't want that at all.

"Here, and thanks," she said, holding the phone out to him.

His fingers brushed hers as he took the small

case, and she jerked back, thankful that he had a hold on the phone before she reacted.

"Can I suggest something?" He moved back a half pace, leaning his hips against a gunmetal gray Mercedes convertible behind him.

"What is it?"

"I've got a car. I'll drive you to your hotel. No need to risk your life getting a taxi."

Reasonable, logical Nicholas. Saying things she couldn't rebut, things that made sense, but left her feeling helpless. "I don't know."

"I won't cough on you, I promise."

"You really do look awful," she said without thinking.

He smiled a bit weakly, but it still jolted her slightly. "Thanks, I needed that," he murmured, and as he spoke the smile was gone, replaced by a slight grimace and narrowing of his eyes. "You, on the other hand, look fantastic. Small town life must really agree with you."

"Jensen Pass is not that small," she said, "and you need to sit down."

"I'd be glad to sit, if you'd make up your mind about the ride."

She'd never known him to be sick before, but then again, she hadn't known him for very long. "Maybe I should drive."

She was worried there'd be another smile, but it never came. He passed a hand roughly over his face, then exhaled. "I'll drive," he said, his eyes narrowed even more, as if the harsh light in the garage was bothering him. "You're coming?"

"Yes," she said.

He turned and reached for the door handle of the gray Mercedes he'd been leaning against. A sleek, sports convertible that fit him perfectly. She should have known he'd be driving a car like this. "A new car?"

He opened the door and stood back. "Yes, and I want to keep it in one piece."

"I'm not that bad a—"

He cut her off with a touch on her shoulder. "Get in. We aren't going to argue about your driving skills right now."

His fingers felt hot against her skin, shocking her, and she darted him a look before slipping into the luxurious leather interior and away from his touch. When he got inside with her, a scent she'd forgotten existed surrounded her—that mingling of mellow aftershave Nick always wore and a certain maleness that had always seemed to be all his.

She tried not to inhale too deeply and glanced away from Nick, down at the console between the seats. Something bright caught her attention in a sea of wood tones and leathers. Something small and glittery gold. A present. The size of a ring box. She looked away quickly, but not quick enough. Nick was watching her, but said nothing. She turned from him, realized that her stomach was tight and just stopped herself before she pressed a hand to her middle.

A ring box. Why did the idea of another woman in Nick's life feel so horrible for her? She hadn't been stupid enough to think he'd be without a woman for long. And she certainly wasn't in his life any longer, and as soon as she signed the papers, everything would be done. But she couldn't deny that it hurt a bit to have him heading into another relationship so quickly. Maybe that was why he'd shown up here to get the papers signed despite his being so sick.

She almost jumped out of her skin when he spoke again. "Where to?"

She told him which hotel, then he drove slowly out into the heavy afternoon traffic. Fingering the leather covered steering wheel, he inhaled audibly before speaking again. "So, you're doing good?"

"Yes, and you?"

"Good, fine, busy."

"That's good. You like that, keeping busy."

"Sometimes." He rubbed the back of his neck and rotated his head slowly. "Today I could have used a calmer agenda."

"Been in court all day?"

He cast her a sideways glance, the hazel eyes muffled by the dark lashes and the way his lids lowered slightly. "All day. Three cases." He looked away. "I really messed up one case. The guy's going to trial and I should have been able to cut a deal."

Déjà vu. This could have been happening last summer, Nick tired from court, her listening to him, watching him wind down, then having her time with him. She stopped the thoughts, veering away from how they spent their time together. "I'm sure you'll get him off even if it goes to trial," she said. "Even if he's a serial killer."

"No serial killer," Nick said.

"What did he do, burglary, rape, terrorism?"

"Bad checks."

"Oh," she said, biting her lip, killing a strange urge to laugh.

"Oh? That's it?"

She looked at him now, and was startled at how tense he looked. His jaw was set and the brackets at his mouth were deeper with no trace of humor. It killed any laughter in her. "What do you want me to say? Is he innocent? I didn't think that was a consideration for you. I wasn't innocent."

"No, you weren't, were you?"

"Not even close. I didn't mean to do anything, but I did it. I did it for good reasons, but that didn't matter, did it?"

The traffic came to a dead stop before they reached the freeway. "We all do things for good reasons, then realize that we've messed up big time," he said.

She looked away from him, his words too close to the past for her comfort. "I'm not so unique, am I?"

"Don't underestimate yourself," he muttered.

She looked back at him as he ran his hand over his face and she could see a thin film of moisture on his skin. "Nick, are you—?"

He hit the steering wheel with the flat of his hand, cutting off her words at the same time a siren sounded outside. "Just what I need," he ground out as he stopped the car.

It was then she realized how crowded the street was and the fact that no one was moving except for a police car with its siren going, weaving in and out of the cars on the clogged street. The sirens wailed, then faded off as the squad car headed west and Nick reached for his cell phone. She had no idea who he called, but she heard him say where they were, then ask what was going on. He listened, then closed the phone and dropped it on the console.

"What is it?" she asked, straining to see in front of them.

"We aren't going to be able to go this way for quite a while." He sank back in the seat and exhaled. "There's an incident near the freeway, and the police have the area shut down completely."

"An incident?" she asked.

He looked around as he spoke. "Probably a standoff or an arrest or the ever popular slow speed chase. Whatever it is, the whole place is shut down tight."

"You could get a new client, maybe," she said.

The joke fell flat as he darted her a sharp glance. "I'll leave that up to the ambulance chasers," he said tightly, then turned toward her, his arm moving in her direction.

She wondered if he was going to put his arm around her. But was incredibly relieved when he gripped the back of her seat, twisted and looked behind him. "We'll find an alternate route," he said as he eased out of their lane, and off onto a side street.

She watched him, not missing the way he pinched the bridge of his nose between his thumb and forefinger, or the way he kept exhaling heavily. "Nick, you're sick. Just let me drive."

He glanced at her, those hazel eyes narrowed on her. "I'm sick, not crazy," he said, but softened his words with a slight smile. "I'm also dying of thirst."

"Then stop for a drink, and I can take a cab." She spotted a row of small restaurants ahead of them. "Just stop at one of them, and I'll find a cab."

"Not a bad idea," he said almost under his breath as he eased the car to the side of the street.

Sam looked to her right and saw he'd stopped in front of a small Italian restaurant with valet parking. An attendant was at the driver's side before the car completely came to a stop.

"Okay," she said, wishing she wasn't so aware of the very faint shadow of a new beard at his jawline. "I can call a cab from the restaurant," she said.

He turned around, shifting to grip the steering wheel with both hands, but his eyes never left her. "Sure, whatever. Let's just get inside, okay?"

She found herself nodding. "Okay, sure." It was obvious he really needed to sit and relax.

By the time she was on the sidewalk, he was coming toward her. He didn't touch her, but moved by her close enough to lightly brush her arm as he started for the entrance. "Come on."

She looked at the restaurant. The building appeared "old worldish" with worn bricks on the exterior, heavy wood accents, and a cobbled entrance walk. It wasn't like the high end places that they had frequented most of the time when they'd been married. Nothing like the restaurant in downtown near the courthouse where they'd had their first date, a date that had ended with Nick wanting to make love to her. She'd wanted it too after only four hours. That was the sort of hold this man could have over her if she let her guard down.

She stepped into the dimly lit space. The fragrance of savory food was everywhere, soft music filtered in from hidden speakers and the murmur of voices from a handful of customers was subdued. A man bowed slightly to them. "Welcome. Two?"

Nick nodded, and the man showed them to a small table near an empty fireplace. As they sat down opposite each other, Nick laid his cell phone on the table and sank back in the chair. His expression seemed tight, and she didn't miss the way he rubbed his hand over his face again.

"A bottle of Cabernet and some ice water," he said without looking at the man hovering near the table.

"Yes, sir, right away," he said and scurried off.

Sam almost asked Nick how he felt, but bit her tongue. It wasn't her business. He wasn't her business. She felt as tight as a coiled spring and almost jumped out of her skin when Nick spoke.

"Relax, I'm not going to bite you."

She darted a look up, thankful he wasn't smiling. Then again, he wasn't frowning either. Actually, he was watching someone behind her. Before she could glance back, the waiter was there with a bottle of wine and a carafe of icy water.

He carefully poured a taste of wine for Nick in

one of the goblets on the table, then when Nick tasted it and nodded, he filled both goblets. "I will be right back," the waiter said after filling their water goblets.

Nick reached into his pocket and took out a medicine bottle. He shook out one small white pill, reached for the water goblet and tossed the pill into his mouth. As he sipped the cool water, he glanced at Sam, then put down the goblet and the medicine bottle. "They've got good wine here," he said as he reached for his glass. "Try it."

"No, thanks, I need to get going." She motioned to his cell phone. "I'll call a cab."

He reached for the phone with his free hand, but instead of picking it up and handing it to her, he just fingered it where it lay. "Don't go."

He drew his hand back, releasing the phone if she wanted to reach out and take it. Then he took another drink of his wine. "Sorry. Go ahead and make your call."

She hesitated, uneasy about his paleness and the way his eyes seemed a bit glossy. "Nick, if you don't feel well, I can stay for a few minutes." She had no idea why she made that offer when she should be leaving and making her escape. But she felt the need to add, "I can stay until you feel okay to drive, if you need me."

"If I need you?" He exhaled roughly, then reached for his glass again. "It's too late for that," he muttered, those hazel eyes narrowed on her, shadowed by the dim lighting in the restaurant.

Then he said something so low that she wasn't certain she'd heard correctly. "I never stopped."

## Chapter Four

Nick couldn't believe what he was thinking. Everything was getting hazy, but his thoughts were clear. Just his looking at Sam across the table—even though he felt like death warmed over—confirmed that he'd never stopped wanting her.

"What did you say?" Sam asked.

"I…I said it's too late." He took another drink, unable to keep looking at her and think at all. "And it is." The wine was spreading warmth in his middle, the only warmth he could feel at that moment. "Why, what did you think I said?"

"I thought…" She shrugged. "Nothing. I need to call a cab."

He didn't want her to leave. She couldn't.

"Why can't I?" she asked, shocking him that he'd said what he thought without even realizing it. He was sicker than he realized, or the medication was doing crazy things to his mind.

"You can leave," he said. "Of course you can. But taste the wine first. It's great."

She looked at the glass she hadn't yet touched. "Wine is wine," she said.

"You're dead wrong. Wine isn't just wine. This is excellent wine."

She touched the goblet but didn't pick it up. Instead, she looked around the small room. "Have you been here before?"

"I don't know, but it looks familiar. Or maybe it's like a lot of other restaurants." He sipped more wine. "They tend to blur in my mind after a while."

"You still don't eat at home?" she asked.

"Not if I can help it," he said, and remembered her attempts at cooking. She'd burned everything. "How's your cooking?"

"I can boil water now," she said, and the shadow of a smile at her lips made his head swim.

"Oh, a big stride in your culinary talents," he said.

"Big strides. Boiling water. Toasting toast. Making orange juice from concentrate." He couldn't look away from the smile that touched her eyes. It was giving him crazy ideas, throwing him back to the past, to a time when he could reach across the table and stroke her cheek, smile back at her and know they'd leave without touching their drinks. They'd leave and make love far into the night.

He watched her very carefully, not sure if he'd said anything that time or not. But she wasn't getting ready to hit him, she wasn't laughing and she wasn't running out of the place. He very carefully said, "I'm impressed. Orange juice concentrate. Big-time cooking."

She lifted the goblet and took a sip, then said, "Don't be too impressed. I still can't figure out the microwave."

He cradled his wineglass and studied her intently. "Cars and microwaves," he murmured.

"That's the beginning of the list," she said. "You can add washers and dryers to that list, too."

"Don't do that," he said softly.

"Do what?"

"Run yourself down. Why don't you say that you paint pictures that are…enchanting?"

Her eyes widened slightly. Yes, he'd said that out loud. And that was good because he really meant it. Her pictures had been enchanting, as enchanting as their creator.

"You think so?"

"Yes, I do." He finished the wine in his glass. "You're a talented artist."

She looked uncomfortable, but he was sure that he'd complimented her…and meant it.

"A starving artist," she said.

Her image began to soften and blur in front of him. She was beginning to look almost as ethereal and magical as her paintings. "Are you okay for money?" he asked.

"That was a figure of speech," she said quickly. "I'm fine. I'm not asking for any money in the divorce."

He hadn't meant to imply that, or make her frown, either. He'd offended her somehow and hated doing it. "I know. I was just thinking. When we met, you were broke, and when you left, you didn't take much."

"I had the same as when we got married. That's fair."

"That isn't what I meant. I don't want you to be wanting for anything." It was the least he could do for her.

"I won't starve as long as there's peanut butter. I've got a roof over my head and I've got prospects." Her chin lifted slightly. "I'm fine."

"Are you happy?" He'd said the wrong thing again without evening thinking. It was the damned medicine. His thoughts became words before he could stop them. And he'd offended her. He could tell by the way she carefully put her glass on the table. "I really need to get going," she said.

"Are you?" he asked, suddenly needing to know.

"Am I what?"

"Happy."

"Yes, I'm happy. I'm fine. I'm good. And I'm going," she said. "Thanks for the excellent wine." She was frowning again. "And you'd better take a cab home."

"I'll be okay," he said, a real lie, but he wasn't about to tell her that she was starting to float in front of his eyes. "I'll just get the bill, then get along myself."

Sam wanted out of there, and she wanted out now. She didn't want to hear him say anything about her work being magical, or have him ask if she needed money, or if she was happy. She didn't want him looking at her as if he was really interested. Why did he have to look at her as if what she said was the most important thing in the world?

She was about to rise from the table when the waiter came back and started telling them about the specials of the day. The man was looking at her expectantly with a pad in his hand, and she realized he was waiting for her to order. "I...I'm leaving. I'm sorry."

He looked at Nick. "How about you, sir?"

"Nothing. Just bring the bill, please," he said.

She glanced at Nick. He really didn't look well. There was a paleness still clinging to him, and his eyes were narrowed oddly. "Do you still have your headache?"

He exhaled. "A bit. I hate being sick."

Any other nearly ex-wife would have nodded and agreed that they remembered how he hated being sick, but she had never seen Nick when he'd been ill. Their time together had been so brief there were a lot of things they'd never done or experienced together.

"Sorry you're sick," she said, uncertain what to do next.

"Me too," he said with another grimace. "Tell me something," he said, fingering his empty glass and making no move to refill it.

"What?"

"Was it worth it?"

"What?"

"Us. Everything." He leaned forward, pushing his glass away toward the edge of the table. "Would...would you do it all over again?"

If he'd loved her, she would have gone through anything. But would she do it all over again knowing what she did now? "Would it end differently?"

"How...differently?" he asked, almost mumbling now. "What...what would it have taken...to make it work?"

This conversation was stupid, going places she didn't ever want to go. But she couldn't help herself. "Nothing could have made it work. You weren't about to go to prison—your term for marriage.'' She couldn't say, ''If you loved me,'' so she said, ''I wasn't about to live a nothing life.''

He studied her hard for a long moment. ''A nothing life? What in the hell does that mean?''

A life without love. But she hedged. ''Doing whatever we wanted to do whenever we wanted to do it, and not thinking about the future or building anything.'' Her hands were clenched, and she had to force them open on the tabletop. ''We didn't build anything, Nick. We just existed.''

''Existed? That's what you call what we had? Existing?''

''I'm sorry. I didn't want to talk about this. You don't feel well and I have to get back to my hotel.''

''You're always the one leaving,'' he said, and almost looked shocked at his words. But he didn't apologize.

''Yes, I guess I am,'' she whispered. ''I have to.''

His jaw tightened. ''You know what? I forget why you left. You were just gone.''

''Nick, don't,'' she said, hating the way he put her on the defensive.

''Don't do what?''

''Turn everything around. You're not in court. I'm not some witness you're trying to unnerve with your cross-examination.''

''I unnerve you?''

"No…yes…you just never…" She bit her lip hard.

"I thought there was a time when I could—" he paused suggestively "—unnerve you."

She flashed him what she hoped was a withering gaze. "And don't do that."

He lifted one eyebrow in her direction. "What?"

"Treat me like some stupid witness you can play word games with."

"I've thought of you as a lot of things, but not a stupid witness."

It went from bad to worse. Her stomach was clenching so hard it ached. She abruptly pushed back from the table and got to her feet. Without looking at Nick, she headed for the back hallway with the sign, Rest Rooms, posted on the wall.

A mistake. A horrible mistake. She should have sat in her car and waited for the rental company to bring a replacement vehicle. She shouldn't have gone to Danforth's offices. Hell, she shouldn't have even come to Los Angeles. A string of errors that was now making her pay dearly. She went quickly down the dimly lit hallway to the ladies' room, then hurried inside. She flicked on the light, closed the door and leaned weakly back against it.

She closed her eyes, fully aware that everything she believed to be true was a lie. She wasn't over Nick. She wasn't immune to Nick on any level, and she couldn't go out and talk to him even for the short time it would take to get a cab. She'd been a real fool when she first met him and she was still a fool.

She crossed to the vanity and saw a pay phone on the wall. She was getting a taxi and leaving…now. She started for the phone but stopped when someone rapped on the outer door. She opened it to see the waiter standing there.

"Madam, the gentleman you're with," he said in a discreet whisper as he leaned toward her, "he…he isn't feeling well. I believe there's a problem."

Sam looked over at their table and even from this distance could see that there was something wrong. Two men seemed to be holding Nick up as if they were keeping him from falling.

She hurried across the room and instinctively reached out to Nick. Touching his hand, she found it so cold and damp that it jarred her. "Nick, what's the matter?" she asked.

Nick's hazel eyes darted in her direction, but they looked as if they couldn't quite focus on her. "Damn, I…" His tongue touched his lips. "I jush…I…" He moved from the two men's support to grip the back of his chair, then slowly, carefully, sank back into his seat. With a long, shaky release of breath, he hunched forward and buried his face in his hands.

He really was sick. "Do you need a doctor?" she asked, bending over him but stopping herself from reaching out to touch him again.

"No," he said, his voice muffled by his hands. "I jush…jus…" He took another breath. "Give me…time."

Then it hit her. He couldn't even form a simple sentence. The man was drunk! She didn't know how, but he was almost falling-down drunk. "You're drunk," she accused, as she dropped back into her seat and stared at him across the tabletop.

That made him lift his head, and his eyes looked even less focused now. "Drunk? No…on wine? I…no…light-headed…sick. I jush tried to…to shta…" He frowned. "I mish…miscalculated my step when I stood."

"Nick, you're drunk," she said softly.

"Not hardly." He shook his head, then reached for the medicine bottle he'd left on the table. "I'm sick." Before she realized what he was doing, he began trying to open the bottle to take more medication, but he couldn't make the top snap off. He dropped the bottle back onto the table, cursed under his breath, then muttered, "Sick…very sick. Flu…or shumthing."

"Something," she said, correcting him. "That something is drunk."

"Sick," he repeated slowly. "Damned sick."

"Okay, sick, but how much did you have to drink earlier?"

"Nothing. I didn't even have lunsh." He grimaced. "Lunch," he enunciated carefully, looking annoyed. "God, I'm...it's blurring. The...the room..." He closed his eyes and leaned forward, burying his face in his hands again.

"Is there anything I can do?" the waiter asked as he hovered behind Nick. "Perhaps some black coffee?"

She stared at Nick as she shook her head and motioned the man away with one hand. "I'm driving you home. Whatever's going on, you need to sleep it off."

Even as drunk or sick as he was, she didn't miss the vague look of uneasiness in his eyes when he looked up at her. "You...drive my car?"

"Oh, come on. I'm doing better," she said, making light of her horrendous driving record. "I haven't been in court for—" she stumbled over that "—a while, and I'll be very careful. Besides, you've got insurance."

"I'd rather not...not use it," he muttered thickly.

"Well, we can take a taxi, leave your wonderful car here, abandoned in Los Angeles or...let me drive you home?" He was looking at her as if she'd suggested they go and find an alien spaceship to take him home. And she would have laughed if he hadn't looked so terrible. "Nick, you can't drive. And your car wouldn't stand a chance if you left it around here overnight."

"It's in valet parking, and that's safe." He swallowed hard. "It's safe."

"Whatever," she said. "It's your car, and I won't point out that valet parking around here means they put it on a side street. You know what you're doing, and as I said, you've got insurance."

"Know what, Sam?" he breathed. "You should've been an attorney."

"No thanks. There are enough sharks in the sea, and I'll call a taxi for both of us."

He stared at her, then pressed both hands flat on the table. "Okay, okay, you win. You'll be careful and…no…no crazy turns?"

"And no blown tires." She crossed her heart. "Promise."

"If I washn't…so…sick…" He sat back, exhaled roughly. "Okay."

She knew what it cost him to let her drive, so she didn't waste any time. "Let's go."

"I'm crazy," he mumbled.

"You're sick and a bit drunk," she said, taking some money out of her purse and laying it on the table, then holding her hand out to him. "And we're leaving."

He stared at her hand for the longest time, then his hand was in hers, his strong fingers gripping her for support as he got slowly, carefully, to his feet. She could feel how unsteady he was, and her breath caught when he easily slipped his arm around her shoulders and leaned against her.

For one crazy moment she was back in the past, with Nick holding her, his scent surrounding her, the heat of him seeping into her soul. Then the moment was gone. She was supporting a drunk man who had to get home. A man who would be nothing to her as soon as she signed some papers.

That thought jolted her back to reality, and with Nick leaning against her, they made their way awkwardly toward the exit. One of the waiters was there, taking Nick by his other arm. "Ma'am, your car's being brought around," he said to her.

"Thanks," she replied as they left and stepped onto the sidewalk by the valet parking station. The Mercedes soon pulled up to the curb, and she eased herself away from Nick to go around and get into the car. She realized she hadn't been breathing very deeply while he'd been so close. Was she afraid of inhaling his scent? She didn't know. But she knew she was relieved when the waiter helped Nick into the car while she slid in behind the wheel.

"Ma'am?" She turned to see Nick settling in his seat and the waiter who had helped him looking at her. He held out the medicine bottle. "Don't forget this, ma'am," he said.

Sam took the item and placed it on the console by the foil-wrapped ring box she'd forgotten about. She reached into her purse and handed the waiter a folded bill. "Thank you so much."

He smiled and said, "Hope things will be okay," then moved back and swung the passenger door shut.

She turned her attention to the dashboard. The car was luxurious, with enough bells and whistles to confuse a jet pilot. Thank goodness the key was in the ignition and the engine was idling. She knew where the gearshift was, put it in Drive, then eased away from the curb and into traffic.

Nick sighed, and she glanced at him to see his eyes were closed and he'd relaxed against the headrest. The world had suddenly narrowed to just the two of them, and that loss of the ability to breathe deeply was there again. She turned from Nick and tried to focus on driving, ignoring the tightness in her chest.

"The traffic's better," she said to break the silence and take her mind off everything else.

"Jush…just take…it easy," he whispered.

She stared at the cars ahead of her and realized she didn't even know where he lived now. "Where to?" she asked.

"Malibu. Home."

The single word hung between them, the full impact not lost on her. He hadn't moved out of the home she'd thought she'd found with him. A place that turned out to be just a stopover like the foster homes. How she had loved the place on the ocean, cantilevered out over the beach far below. Windows everywhere. She cut the nostalgia off quickly and said, "Okay." And hoped she remembered how to get there.

She headed west, searching for a sign for the Coast Highway while Nick stayed silent in the seat beside her. When she spotted the sign and knew she was on the right track, she turned to Nick. But before she could say anything, there was a flash, and she looked at the road ahead just in time to see a car cut right in front of her.

# Chapter Five

"Oh, no!" Sam gasped as she stood on the brakes and felt them pulsate under her foot. Amazingly, there was no impact, and without even anything as dramatic as a squeal of tires, Nick's new car actually stopped inches from the back bumper of the older sedan.

Her heart was hammering, and the sound of Nick's slurred voice didn't help. "Obviously, you haven't changed."

She darted him a look and found him struggling to sit up, gripping the door handle with one hand and the console front with the other.

"It's okay. We didn't hit anything. Just sit back and relax."

"Easy for you to say," he muttered thickly, and sank back in his seat though he didn't let go of his grip on the door and console.

"It's that driver. He's crazy, just shooting out like that and stopping, and I—"

"Haven't changed at all," he grumbled.

She looked away, not wanting to see the line of his jaw or how his hair clung damply at his temples. No, she didn't want to be aware of anything but driving and getting him to bed. No, not bed. She fingered the steering wheel, thankful when the car in front of her started moving again. She cautiously followed until she could turn north onto the four-lane highway that hugged the coast.

Thankfully, Nick stayed silent for the rest of the drive and she never even chanced a look at him. Keeping her gaze straight, she realized that she did remember the way to his house. She spotted stone pillars that marked the turn off the highway onto a side road that ran down toward the beach, then swung to parallel the shoreline on shallow bluffs.

She turned left onto the narrow street to the expansive bluff area where a handful of houses had been built. She drove carefully around an outcropping that forced the road to the edge of the bluffs, then finally saw Nick's house.

She had never even thought of what her reaction would be, if any, to seeing the house again. The last time she'd glimpsed it, it had been through the rear window of the taxi when she was leaving. Then, the sun had been brilliant on the clapboard siding of the single-storied structure and glinted off the multipaned windows.

Now, the last rays of the setting sun bathed it in

a mellow light, turning the windows to liquid gold and making the clinging moisture glisten on the natural-wood clapboards. A light breeze stirred the trees to the east of the house.

She didn't expect to feel such a wrench in her chest at the sight of the house or to experience a totally illogical sense of returning from a long journey. She wasn't "returning" at all. She couldn't go back even though she was physically driving toward the house once again. She slowed to a crawl as she approached the semicircular drive.

She glanced around the car's interior, spotted the garage door opener and used it. The door rose slowly, and she drove the Mercedes into the cavernous space that angled down and under the main house. She stopped, switched off the engine and turned to Nick.

She'd thought he'd fallen asleep and was jolted to find him staring at her, his expression unreadable. "You're home in one piece," she said, reaching for the door handle.

"Barely," she heard him whisper as she got out. She would have headed right for the phone to call a cab if Nick hadn't stopped her. "I could...I could use some help here."

His voice was low and thick, but it echoed in the spacious garage. She turned and faced Nick. He was out of the car and standing but gripping the top of the open door—a grip so tight that his knuckles were white.

She didn't want to go inside any farther than the small utility room where the phone was, but she knew Nick would never make it inside on his own. Bracing herself, she went around to Nick. He put his arm around her shoulders as if it was the most natural thing in the world.

She eased her arm around his waist, ignoring the feeling of closeness that all but choked her, then closed her eyes for a fleeting moment before slowly helping Nick to the back door. She opened the door and entered the house through the utility room. Still holding on to each other, they went into the kitchen, a room touched by the light of the setting sun shining through a wall of windows.

She'd barely used this room when she lived here, except on some early mornings when they'd sit at the table and watch dawn touch the sky. That memory saddened her and she turned from it, slowly making her way with Nick across the tile floor and through the swinging doors into the main part of the house.

She felt as if she'd stepped back in time, into the painfully modern room. The floor-to-ceiling glass doors were ajar, opening onto the sweeping deck at the back of the house. And as she knew from experience, anyone in this room could hear whatever was being said out there when the doors were open.

Another memory to turn away from, and she did. Yet even as she helped Nick ease down onto the long leather couch, she couldn't block out another echo from the past.

She'd been standing at the doors to the deck after Greg had left with some mumbled excuse. She and Nick had been facing each other though neither had spoken for a long moment. Then she'd found the words from somewhere deep inside her.

"You've never told me you love me," she'd said in a voice she barely recognized as her own.

He'd looked at her, then reached out for her, but she'd moved back. If he'd touched her, she wasn't sure what would have happened.

"Sam, you know I care about you. I wouldn't be here now if I didn't care."

She'd cut him off. "You don't love me, do you?"

He'd turned his back to her to stare outside. "Oh, hell, I care about you. I don't know about love, if it even exists."

The words still echoed inside her, as painful as they'd been months ago, the pain growing when she realized how much she could have loved him. How much she'd wanted to love him and have him love her. "Why did you marry me?" she'd whispered.

That was when he'd faced her and said bluntly, "I didn't have a choice, did I?" But she'd had a choice then. And she'd chosen to leave.

She looked down at Nick as he sank weakly into the supple black leather cushions. And she had a choice now.

Despite everything, the man touched her when he hunched forward, burying his face in his hands. "Oh, man," he groaned.

She stood over him, fighting concern about his condition and the natural instinct to do something else for him. But she had to get out of here. "I'll call a cab," she said. "I can use the phone in the kitchen."

He raked his fingers through his hair, then he was looking up at her. "Could…could you get me my…my medicine before you go?" he asked in a low voice. "And could you bring me some water, too?"

"Sure, of course," she said, and hurried to get the medicine and her things out of Nick's car. She left her purse and documents in the utility room then went through the kitchen, found a bottle of water for Nick and headed back into the living area.

Nick was still on the couch, but he was lying down now, stretching his long frame out on the cushions, his head against the arm. His eyes were closed. She started to open the medicine bottle to take out a pill for him. But she stopped when she saw a small yellow sticker on the bottle. "Do not mix with alcohol. Can produce drowsiness, faulty coordination, unconsciousness."

She looked back at Nick. "Nick, this medicine..."

He stirred but didn't open his eyes. "For...for flu...sick," he muttered thickly.

She crouched down beside him and said, "It says you aren't supposed to drink alcohol with it. If you do, there can be complications."

That brought an odd, lopsided smile from him. "Like making me...?" He swallowed. "Making...me...drunk?"

"I think so," she whispered, but not totally certain that was all the combination could do to him. "I'll be right back," she said and, carrying the medicine bottle, went into the kitchen and found the phone.

Quickly, she dialed the pharmacy number on the bottle and talked to one of the pharmacists. After she explained what had happened, he asked several questions, then finally assured her that Nick might have a hangover in the morning, but if he was coherent now, he'd be okay.

She thanked him for his help, hung up and went back to Nick. He was still lying there, looking so incredibly peaceful and so incredibly sexy. Damn it, his effect on her just never stopped, and she was thankful he was asleep. She didn't want to look into those hazel eyes again. She wanted to leave, to have everything over and done with, but before she understood her own actions, she bent closer to him.

A goodbye, a simple goodbye that she hadn't told him the last time. Then, she'd turned and walked away. And he hadn't tried to stop her. Now he was asleep. He wouldn't ever know the goodbye had been said. But she would. She'd remember, and she knew that she needed that final tie broken.

"Goodbye," she whispered, leaning close to his ear. She touched Nick on the shoulder, ignoring the way her hand shook when she felt the heat of his body under her fingertips. "Goodbye."

NICK WAS FLOATING in a soft place that had no sharp edges, no discomfort. Softness everywhere, even Sam's voice surrounding him, whispering, but he couldn't tell what she was saying. Then he felt a touch, her touch, and he reached toward it. There was more softness, but it was mixed with heat and silk. And the aching need that he knew had been there from the first engulfed him. He had ahold of her, the dream so real he could feel the trembling in her body. Then she was over him, and he let himself go. He found her lips, the dreams solidifying with the taste of her invading him.

Dream or not, he needed it beyond measure and

he fell farther and farther into it, taking what he could, and finding the reality of Sam again. The taste of her in his mouth, the heat of her all around him, the scent of her filling him, filtering into his soul. A dream, and he was so thankful for it his heart hurt.

Nothing mattered. The past was gone. The pain was gone. There was just Sam. Sam, everywhere. And urgency beyond measure. She was over him, her image blurred and shimmering, her hands on him. The barrier of his shirt was gone, and he felt her touch on his bare skin. Her fingers trailed over his chest, and lower, to his belt.

Then she was beside him on the couch, caught between his body and the leather cushions. He fumbled with the zipper on her dress, his fingers awkward even in the dream. Then the material was gone, and he felt her. He really felt her for the first time in what could have been an eternity. He felt the silk and heat of her skin. He heard the fragile material of her bra give as he tugged at it, then he felt her breast in his hand.

When he bent and found her nipple with his mouth, he heard her moan. The sound echoed through his being, filling him with life, banishing thought and reason. He tasted her skin, teased her nipple with his tongue, relishing the fantasy of her gasping and the low, animalistic moans he'd conjured up in the dream.

He trailed his tongue on her skin, filling himself with her essence, and all the while he was dreaming that she was tugging at his shirt, taking it off and tossing it somewhere into the shadows all around them. Then she arched toward him, and he shifted again. The next thing he knew she was under him, naked. Every inch of her shadowed, yet he knew the hollows and curves. He knew the heat and moistness.

He tangled his legs with hers, felt her arms circle his neck, felt her pushing against him, and his desire, even in the dream, throbbed. There was freedom and need, a potent combination, and he claimed them both. He touched her with his hardness, felt the silky heat, and her hips lifted.

She was moist and ready. He told himself he heard her saying, "Oh, please, just love me." The words drifted to him, filled him. He entered her, experiencing a pleasure so keen that it made him tremble. He eased himself in until he could go no deeper. He was connected. He was anchored. He was whole.

Then the sensation of pleasure came in shards of ecstasy that ripped through him, killing him and healing him at the same time. They found his soul and claimed it, and in one burst of pure bliss, he found his goal. He knew what he'd needed all his life. He knew the meaning of happiness, of completeness and satisfaction. He knew the purpose of his life, and it was all in a dream.

A dream where he settled into the softness again, felt the beating of another's heart against his side. Felt the touch of someone on his chest and heard the soft sounds of crying coming out of the shadows. He hushed the sobbing, holding tightly to the trembling heat against him, then the dream dissolved into nothingness.

SAM COULD FEEL her heart breaking.

She stayed very still, caught between the leather of the couch cushions and Nick. His body was against her, their heat mingling, his leg heavy over her bare thighs, and she couldn't stop crying.

She still loved him. And in that moment, she knew she would always love him. But she'd never have this with him again. He wanted her now, he needed her now, but he didn't love her. If they could stay like this forever, things would be okay. But sooner or later, the real world would come back into focus, and then there would be nothing for them.

She closed her eyes, listening to the beat of his heart against her cheek, letting the feel of him filter into her being. She sealed everything in her soul, then when her tears had dried, she moved. Carefully, awkwardly, she managed to get off the couch. Without looking at Nick, she found her clothes. Forgoing her bra, she stuffed it into her purse and just slipped on her dress.

But she found herself unable to leave. Turning to look at Nick sleeping peacefully, she moved closer. Moonlight shining through the window cast sharp shadows at his jaw and eyes.

She somehow kept herself from touching him one last time, remembering what that ''last'' touch had just cost her. She finally walked away from him through the shadows of the room to the back of the house. But she didn't go into what had once been their bedroom. She couldn't. Instead, she grabbed a blanket from the guest bedroom and went back to lay it over a still-sleeping Nick.

In the utility room, she collected her purse and envelope, stopping a moment to call for a cab. Then, looking down at the envelope in her hand, she knew that she had to sign the papers now. Quickly, she penned her name to the divorce agreement, put the papers back in the envelope, then went to the kitchen and placed it on the counter.

She slipped out the side door and into the night. It was over…finally over.

NICK WOKE SUDDENLY to the light of early morning flooding the house. He rested his forearm over his eyes and stretched, thankful his headache from last night was gone. Then he realized he didn't remember coming home. No, that wasn't true. Sam and he had been at the restaurant, then in the car. He sat up abruptly. Sam.

He felt the cool air of morning brush his skin as the blanket fell away and he realized he was totally naked. Then he saw his clothes scattered on the floor by the couch. The house was silent, no sounds save the crashing of the waves far below.

Slowly, he sank back, tugged the blanket up over him and stared at the ceiling. The flu or whatever he'd had was gone. No headache. No aches at all. Just a lethargy that made it easy for him to lie there and try to make sense of last night.

Him and Sam. Him wanting her. No, that was a dream, the dream he always had. But no, it wasn't quite the same at all. He had been with her last night, her voice in the car beside him. He glanced over to see his medicine bottle on the coffee table.

He tossed off the blanket, stood and paused for just a moment to get his balance. Then he padded across the floor to the utility room. Opening the door to the garage, he saw his Mercedes was safely parked inside. He'd obviously driven home and just didn't remember.

Going into the kitchen, Nick turned on the faucet and splashed cold water over his face. Damn it, he couldn't figure out what had happened. He'd left Danforth's offices. He and Sam had gone to the restaurant. But that was where everything blurred and started to fade.

He grabbed some towels, pressed them to his face, then tossed them onto the counter and went back into the living room. As he neared the couch, he let out a gasp when he stepped on something. Looking down, he saw the morning sunlight glinting off something small on the polished wood floor.

He bent down to pick up a delicate locket. He had a clear image of Sam fingering it at her throat in Danforth's offices. The heart-shaped locket gleamed in the sunlight, almost painful to his eyes, and he closed his fingers around the delicate piece of jewelry.

Sam had been here. That part was true. Sam. In the house again. But when he tried to remember her here, it all flipped and slid into the dream. Nick could feel his body tighten as the memory came to him—the fantasy of his dream. Or was it a dream? His body certainly wasn't acting as if it had been a dream. He could recall the soft echoes of her voice in his ear, the sense of being surrounded by her.

And as he entered the kitchen once more, he saw an envelope. Opening it, he knew immediately what was inside. The divorce papers.

The sight of Sam's signature at the bottom knotted his stomach. She'd driven him home, signed the papers and left. That was what had happened, not some delusional dream.

His curse echoed through the house. Turning from the papers and the locket, Nick headed for the other side of the house. He had work to catch up on after being sick. Sam was his past—her signature on the divorce papers only underscored that fact. Their marriage was over. The mistake was corrected. Despite his lingering needs, his past with Sam was gone. Now it was time to get on with the rest of his life.

# Chapter Six

*Four months later*
*San Francisco*

The phone rang in one of the plush corporate suites in the San Francisco hotel. The sound was as subtle as the decor in the sitting area. Nick sank back in his chair, reached for the phone and exhaled before speaking. He'd been in the city working nonstop for two days and he was about to go take a deposition from a witness in an important case. He didn't need more problems or more work.

"Viera here."

"Oh, good, I caught up with you," Greg said in his ear, his tone one of obvious relief. "You've been out every time I've tried and your cell's going to your voice mail."

"Well, you caught me. So what's going on?" He could hear the impatience in his voice, and it annoyed him. But he hadn't been sleeping well and his work had been choking him lately.

"No deposition. He's backed out."

"Damn it," Nick muttered and sat forward, pressing the heel of his hand against his forehead. "Are you sure?"

"He's rejected every question you submitted. So we're back at square one."

Nick tossed his pen on the tabletop and exhaled harshly. "Okay, I'm on my way home."

"Not so fast. In case you haven't noticed, you're socked in."

Nick looked out the window ten stories above the city. Heavy fog blocked the view and hung low in the sky. He hadn't noticed. He'd been awake most of the night, tormented by dreams that wouldn't go away. He was tired, so tired.

"There are no flights out," Greg said, "so why don't you just kick back, take a deep breath and keep your scheduled flight tomorrow at noon? You sound a bit stressed even on long distance."

He was stressed, but he hated sitting still. "I'll call later and see if I can get a red-eye out."

"You know what, you probably ought to stay until tomorrow because the guy could change his mind. Or if you come up with different questions, he might go for them. Why waste the trip?"

Because Nick wanted out of the city. He wanted to leave and not look back. But old habits died hard, and for all of his professional life, he'd never let go of a case until it was hopeless. "Okay, you're right. I'll hang out, see what I can come up with and be in touch before I leave tomorrow."

"You should get some sleep."

He wished he could. "Easy for you to say," he grumbled. "I'll be talking to you."

"Sure, take care," Greg said, hanging up.

Nick put down the receiver, then stared at the stack of papers. Enough work. He needed air and the idea of getting in a rental car and just driving was appealing. He snapped open his briefcase, shoving the papers inside. Just as he was about to close it, Nick spotted the small envelope in the side compartment.

It was an insignificant envelope, plain brown with a slight bulge in it. No one would have looked at it twice, but he knew what it contained. And he knew that he'd forgotten to mail it again. He'd blocked its existence out of his mind...again. Sam's locket.

Taking the envelope out of his briefcase, Nick read the address scrawled on the front. Samantha Wells. Her maiden name. And the Jensen Pass address. He stared hard at it, then tossed it back into the briefcase and snapped the case shut, spinning the combination locks. He crossed to the bedroom, kicked off his shoes on the way and headed for the bed, his plan to take a drive now abandoned.

Stripping off his white shirt, he dropped it on the foot of the bed, then stretched out on top of the spread. Rest, he told himself. Just rest. He didn't have to sleep. Just rest. He took several deep breaths and shifted around, settling into the softness of the bed.

Closing his eyes, he took several more slow, even breaths, and the next thing he knew, he was in the dream. It came without the drifting usually that preceded it. That gradual realization that he was lost in the fantasy of being with Sam. This time, he was there, she was there, and he was reaching out to her. He was lost in her. Nothing else mattered. Just Sam.

He sensed the tension, the urgency, but instead of finding release with her, he was wrenched into wakefulness, the sound of his own voice crying out into the air around him. "Sam."

Nick uttered a low curse and got out of bed, crossed to the bathroom and turned on the shower. He stripped off his clothes, then stepped under the cool water that eased his body but did nothing to ease his mind. All because of Sam, because some unconscious part of his mind wouldn't let go of the past.

Crazy, illogical. But then again, every reaction he'd had to the woman had been crazy and illogical. He reached for a sponge and scrubbed his skin, wishing he could go home. But he stopped that thought when he realized that since the night Sam had taken him home, even the house had changed. Sleeping there had been more difficult than in any other place. No, going home wouldn't help.

Getting out of the shower, Nick knew what he needed to do. As crazy as it sounded, he knew that Sam was the one who could let him sleep again. He called down to the desk to ask how far Jensen Pass was from the city. Seventy miles, an easy drive, he was told. After hesitating a moment, Nick asked to have his bill made up and his rental car brought around to the entrance.

He'd drive up to Jensen Pass, give Sam the locket and hope that would bring him closure. Then he'd head back to a hotel closer to the airport, work on new questions for the deposition and leave town tomorrow as planned.

It took longer than he thought to get going, but by late afternoon he was heading north in his rented convertible, putting San Francisco behind him. His briefcase was on the seat beside him, the envelope tucked safely inside. The day was clear and warm, with only a few white clouds dotting the azure sky.

He slowed when he saw a rustic sign pointing toward the coast. Jensen Pass, Est. 1810, Pop. 2,000. Almost immediately, he rounded a bend in the road and saw the town. It had been built into the curve of a harbor, spreading up from a myriad of docks up onto the hills and along the shore in both directions. The place was larger than he thought it would be, but it still looked quaint with white clapboard houses, small stores and patches of open land.

He pulled into a small gas station, parked to one side and saw an attendant by the pumps. The young girl was dressed in a navy uniform, and when she saw him, she smiled brightly. "Hi there. Very, very hot car," she said, eyeing the convertible with appreciation.

"Thanks. Maybe you can help me. I need directions."

"Where to?" After he gave her the address, she scrunched up her face, thought, then snapped her fingers. "Oh, yeah, sure. That's Mrs. Douglas's place, a big old Victorian house that looks real spooky on Halloween."

"I don't think that's right. I'm looking for a Samantha Wells, not Douglas."

"Yeah, Samantha. I didn't know her last name, but she's a renter. She's been in the guest house for a while."

"How do I get there?"

"Straight north, two miles or so, then look for a sign that says Gull's Nest on it, a nickname for that bit of land. Turn left, go, oh, maybe half a mile and you can't miss the place. It's all white and got a picket fence in the front. Really old-fashioned, you know?''

That would fit Sam to a T. Old-fashioned. ''Thanks.'' He was getting back in the car when the girl came to the door and looked down at him.

''So, are you family?''

''Excuse me?''

''I was wondering if you were related to Samantha or a friend or—''

''A friend,'' he said, wishing it could be so. Just being friends with Sam was about as possible as plugging the hole in the *Titanic* with a cork. ''Thanks for your help.''

He gunned the engine and drove out of the station, heading north. Friends with Sam. He pushed that thought aside. He was tired, and his mind wasn't working right. If only he was able to get a good night's sleep, a night without the dreams, maybe he could think straight. But that wasn't going to happen until he finished whatever was left with Sam.

He looked at the briefcase as he drove into a more rural area to the north. Then he saw a hand-carved sign that read Gull's Nest. He turned onto a tree-lined lane, the lacy shadows of the leaves playing over rugged ground that had more than its share of potholes and ruts. Then he saw the house.

It was an old Victorian, all white, with generous amounts of gingerbread trim painted pale blue. The picket fence ran off in both directions, separating the road from a sea of deep green grass. He had barely pulled into the gravel driveway when the door to the house opened and a woman came out onto the porch.

She was tiny, wore a floppy straw hat and held a rake in one hand. It wasn't until Nick stopped the car near the veranda's steps that he realized the woman was much older than he had thought at first glance.

She had to be in her seventies, but she moved like a much younger person as she came down the steps to meet him as he got out of the car.

"Sir, may I help you?" she asked in a strong voice touched with some sort of accent.

"Mrs. Douglas?"

"That's me. Who are you?"

"Nicholas Viera. I'm looking for Samantha Wells."

"Nicholas Viera." She repeated his name, then shook her head as her eyes narrowed behind her glasses. "You're her ex, aren't you?"

He hated the term, but nodded. "We're divorced."

"What are you doing here?" she asked bluntly. "Samantha never said anything about expecting you."

"I just came on the spur of the moment. I was

in San Francisco and..." Why was he explaining things to this woman? "Is she here?"

She didn't answer his question but asked one of her own out of the blue. "You're a lawyer, right?"

"Yes, but—"

"Do you do land rights and that sort of thing? Because I've got this neighbor to the north who wants to cut up his land, put a bunch of cracker-box houses on it and just ruin this place. I want to stop him, you know, legally. Just stop him in his tracks."

"I'm into criminal law. Sorry."

"Well, it *is* criminal what he's doing," she muttered.

"Ma'am, can you just tell me where to find Samantha?"

She looked at him, then said, "Sure, but I don't think I should just let you go there." She cocked her head to one side. "Are you sure you haven't talked to her?"

"Not for a long time."

"Then why are you here?"

He felt as if he was going up against the palace guards...and losing. "I've got something to give her."

"Something else?"

He didn't understand her, and she was making him crazy. Even though she looked elderly and sweet, she was formidable. "I've got a locket that she lost and I wanted to return it to her."

"Haven't you heard of the post office?"

He inhaled deeply, the next best thing to screaming. "I was in the city and had the locket and wanted to make sure she got it back safely. It's the only thing she has left from her mother, and I—"

"Oh, my, yes, so sad. That poor girl. Well, you know all that foster-care thing and being alone." She narrowed her eyes on him again. "Did you know that she used to run away from her foster home in town and come out here to hide at the cottage? The very cottage she's living in today?"

Nick lost his impatience with the woman as he realized she knew more about Sam than he did. He'd never heard about her running away or where she hid. "So, she's living there now?"

"Yes," she said, pointing past him to a turn off the drive. "Just down there."

"Thanks," he said, and started to go back to his car.

"Mr. Viera?"

He turned as he opened the door. "What?"

She hesitated, then shook her head. "Nothing. It's okay."

He got in behind the wheel and looked up at Mrs. Douglas. "Good luck with your neighbor."

"If you hear about a good lawyer who could take a case like that, would you let me know?"

"Yes, ma'am, I'll let you know."

He drove slowly along the path past what looked like apple trees, then saw the cottage right ahead of him.

The house was two-storied but small, with white clapboard siding and high arched windows. The porch wrapped completely around the house, and a variety of flowers trimmed the foundation and the narrow steps leading up to the door. The place looked like something out of one of Sam's paintings, an enchanted cottage. Sam's home now.

He stopped the car near the steps, got out and soon realized he was actually at the back door. The cottage had been built to face the water, and the main entrance was on that side. Not seeing anyone around, Nick headed for the walkway and the front of the cottage.

SAMANTHA WAS ON her front lawn, looking out over the bluff. Her yellow sundress billowed around her in the light breeze, and she grabbed at the fine material, clutching it to her front as she stood on the thick grass that was cool and damp under her bare feet.

Her thoughts had turned to Nick so much in the past few months she almost believed it was his voice she heard calling to her on the late-afternoon breeze. "Samantha?"

She kept her back to him, wishing she was

dreaming and suddenly knowing she wasn't. She could do this. She could face him. When he called out her name again, she braced herself and slowly turned.

For months she'd thought about seeing him again. But nothing had prepared her for the almost physical blow she felt now. The late-afternoon sun touched his face, setting deep shadows at his jaw and eyes. In a short-sleeved, white shirt and far-too-snug, worn jeans, he seemed almost surreal to her. Larger than she remembered, darker, leaner, and more serious.

He had something in his hand, but she didn't attempt to see what it was. She couldn't look away from the man himself. "It's you," she breathed.

He didn't speak again until he came within about five feet of her, deliberately letting his gaze skim over her. "Yes, it's me," he said.

"How did you get here?" she managed to ask in a voice tinged with tightness.

He shrugged, straining the fine material of his shirt across his broad shoulders. "Drove. Asked directions. Simple, actually."

She didn't smile or acknowledge his attempt at sarcastic humor. There was nothing in her that thought anything he said was funny. Instead, she took a breath, trying to fight a light-headedness that had started when he uttered her name. "Why?" she asked.

"I've never been here, so I had to ask." He looked away from her. "You've got a great view here." Those hazel eyes were back on her again and he changed the subject abruptly. "You've let your hair grow some. I like it."

She touched her tongue to her cold lips. "How did you get back here? Mrs. Douglas doesn't let just anyone onto her property."

"She did her best to block me, but she finally let me through." He shrugged again. "She's pretty formidable for being so tiny."

She couldn't stand this small talk, not when he kept staring at her that way. "What are you doing here?" He held something out to her—a brown envelope. "What's that?"

"Yours."

She reached for the envelope and was thankful her hand wasn't shaking when she took it. Letting go of her dress so the skirt billowed and swirled around her bare legs, she fumbled with the flap, then let what was inside slip out onto her palm.

Her locket. She looked at Nick, then back down at the locket in her hand, the gold glinting in the rays of the sun. "I...I thought I'd lost it. Where did you find it?"

"On the floor in the Malibu house. I guess it came off when you helped me inside." He narrowed his eyes at her. "We need to talk about that night, Sam."

She heard his words, and her hand closed over the locket, holding it so tightly that it almost cut into her palm. Not like this. Not now. She wasn't ready. "Why?" she managed to breathe.

"I'm sorry. I never thought about the medication and the wine. I just thought I'd gotten drunk. Sorry for putting you through everything that happened."

She watched him, literally holding her breath, waiting for the next sentence. But when it came, it wasn't what she expected—no "How could we have let that happen" or "It never should have happened." Instead, he shook his head. "I'm a lousy drunk, and I think I'm a lousier one when I'm combining wine and medicine."

She drew her hands back to her middle, all but crushing the envelope she still held. "You didn't know about combining them. How would you?"

"I learned. When I woke the next morning, I was hung over, but I've had worse. I guess I owe you an apology."

No, not that. No apology. "No, of course, you don't."

"Oh, but I do. I should never have said what I did about your driving. My car was unscathed and so was my insurance policy." He almost smiled, the shadow of it flitting at the corners of his mouth. "Your driving's improved."

This was all wrong. It didn't make sense and

she was having a hard time figuring out what to do. "Nick, we...you...you had the flu."

"Yeah, I sure did. I wondered if you'd gotten it, too."

She'd come home sick at heart and the next morning been sick physically. A sickness that had lasted for over a week, then seemed to go away, only to come back over and over again. "I was sick for a while," she said.

"Oh, Sam, I'm sorry about that, too." He smiled then, a wry expression that crinkled the corners of his hazel eyes. "Damn it, why am I always apologizing to you for something? I don't apologize. I never have, but with you..." His composure faltered slightly. "Well, with you it's different. A lot of things were different."

He wasn't going to say anything about that night, and for some reason, the dread she'd had about a confrontation between the two of them turned to vague pain. That encounter had meant everything to her and obviously nothing to him.

He looked away from her, his smile gone as he glanced around, sizing up the house and its surroundings. "Nice," he finally said.

"Thanks," she replied, and eased her hold on the locket. "You didn't have to bring the locket all this way."

"I know. Mrs. Douglas asked me what was wrong with the post office."

"She's...she's very blunt."

"I'd say she is," he agreed, looking back at her. She could barely meet his gaze. "You like it here, Sam?"

"Yes."

"So you used to run away from your foster home and end up here?"

The man could shock her so easily. She'd never told him that. "What?"

"Your guardian at the gate, Mrs. Douglas, told me you came here when you ran away."

She felt tears coming on. An annoying by-product of all the upheaval in her life at the moment. "You had quite a conversation with Mrs. Douglas, didn't you?"

"You've known her a long time?"

"Just since I rented the house. I think her husband was the one who ran me off all those times, but I don't remember her much from back then, just she was so nice." She didn't remember a lot of her childhood. There were too many goodbyes and never any permanent hellos. All her homes in the past blurred together in her memory. Except the cottage. She remembered every detail of it. Then there had been Nick, the home in Malibu...another goodbye.

Nick was talking, and she realized that she had no idea what he'd been saying. She tried to focus but couldn't get past the way he seemed closer now, close enough that she could hear him take a breath.

"Thanks for the locket. It's all I have from…from the past." She slipped it into the pocket of her dress.

In the glow of the afternoon sun, his features were painfully clear. The way his hair curled slightly at the collar of his shirt, the scar that she'd never asked about, the set of his jaw. Instinctively she moved back a bit, turned away to face the water.

"You had a rough time growing up, didn't you?"

She didn't want sympathy from him. She shrugged. "It wasn't that bad," she said with great understatement. "I survived."

"Yes, I guess you did," he said softly.

If he wasn't going to say anything about that night, she wasn't going to either. After months of agonizing over their lovemaking, months of losing sleep trying to figure out what to do about it, this is what it came to. He didn't care. He could leave and that would be it. She wished that was so, but she knew it wasn't. She had to see him again, but for now she'd take her time. Later, when she was more settled, she could contact him.

"So you have people to see, places to go?"

"I guess so," he said. But she knew he wasn't moving. She could feel him right behind her.

Bracing herself, she turned and he was there, his hands thrust into the pockets of his jeans, and she noticed a small cell phone clipped to his belt as he started rocking slightly on the balls of his feet. "What?" she asked, fighting a feeling of light-headedness.

"One more thing?"

She wasn't going to get out of this easily; she could tell from the tension in his jaw and the intensity in his eyes. There was no smile now and she blinked, trying to focus on him. She couldn't understand why his features were blurring slightly or why he seemed to be rocking slowly back and forth. "What...what is it?"

"That last night, when I was drunk or drugged or both...?"

More light-headedness washed over her, and she couldn't say a thing. The world was shifting, starting to undulate under her feet.

"Sam, about that night..." Nick said, and at the same moment, she felt herself falling forward, right into his arms.

## Chapter Seven

Nick had just wanted to say goodbye, to apologize for his stupor of that evening. But he never got the words out. He took a step closer to Samantha, but then she turned as white as a sheet and toppled toward him. The next thing he knew, she was in his arms. "Sam?" She took a shuddering breath, her head pressed into his shoulder. "Sam, what's wrong?"

Her voice was muffled. "I...I'm the one apologizing now. I'm so...so sorry."

"What's going on?" he asked, feeling as if he was being saturated with sensations—the scent of her, her heat, the feel of her against him. God, he'd missed that. He closed his eyes tightly, fighting his response to her that almost choked him. "Sam?"

"I...I just..." He felt her take a trembling breath. "Whew, I'm sorry." She moved back from him, pressing her palms to his chest to give her leverage. If he'd thought she looked pale before, she looked positively ashen now. "I'm okay."

He didn't let her go even when she tried to push farther from him, afraid to take away his support in case she collapsed again. "You look like hell."

Her gaze lifted to his, her eyes stunningly green in the paleness of her face. "Thanks, I needed that," she muttered.

"Wrong choice of words, but you're as pale as a ghost." He shifted his hold on her and with one hand cupped her face. He didn't retreat despite the fact he felt her tense and glimpsed a shadow of real apprehension in her eyes. "You need to sit down."

She bit her lip. "Just let me go," she said.

He hesitated, then slowly drew back from her. He didn't stop to figure out why he hated letting her go so much or why he only then noticed a slight chill in the air.

"You...you wanted to say something, didn't you?"

Although he still doubted she was okay, he found himself replying, "I was just going to apologize for not saying goodbye to you that night. Everything was just a blur."

"What do you mean?" she asked in a slightly breathy voice.

"Well, I remember being at the restaurant, your driving me home, then something about the house, but that's it. Whatever the side effects of mixing wine with that medicine were supposed to be, they could have added memory loss to the list."

She was staring at him, her eyes widened slightly. "You...you don't remember what happened?" she asked.

Nick shook his head. "No, and I don't think I want to. In college I was a lousy drunk. I'd rather not think about my behavior."

She exhaled in a rush, and he tensed, afraid that she might collapse again. But she didn't. She closed her eyes for a long moment, then exhaled once more and looked back at him. "You remember going home?"

"Vaguely, somewhere in the recesses of my mind, but..." He shrugged sharply, not about to mention his erotic dream. "That's about it, except that I needed to come and tell you I hope you find happiness and that you have a good life."

She hesitated, then said something he didn't expect. "Maybe...maybe sometime we can get together and talk. I mean, later. When you've got time."

No, he knew that wasn't going to happen. He couldn't be with her and expect to feel nothing. Even now, he still had the sensation of her falling into his arms. Being with her again was a bad idea. "I don't think so."

"Why?"

He took a breath and said what he knew he had to say to put an end to it. "There's no reason to prolong this whole thing, is there?"

"You really wanted out of it, didn't you?" she asked in a low, husky voice.

"What?"

"That's what you told Greg. I think you said marriage wasn't what you wanted. You wondered who in the hell thought of forever. That marriage was all my idea, not yours."

He'd been drunk that night, but he did remember the conversation. He just didn't remember her being there. "What in the hell are you talking about?"

"The truth. That last night. You and Greg getting drunk on the deck and you regretting everything."

She'd heard his conversation with Greg. He'd never wanted that, never. But he couldn't deny that he'd said those things. "You overheard us?"

Turning from him, Sam faced the distant horizon. "Yes, I heard the two of you."

Nick stared at her back, the sun touching her hair with gold. He'd never wanted to hurt her. Never. But he could see the tightness in her jaw and the way she hugged herself so hard. Instinctively, he reached out and touched her bare shoulder, trying to get her to turn around and look at him. "You weren't supposed to hear all of that."

She shrugged to break the contact and he drew back. "You were almost shouting at Greg. It wasn't a hard conversation to catch. Besides, it doesn't make any difference now, does it?"

This wasn't going the way he'd hoped it would at all. There were bigger gaps opening up, gaps so big that a simple "I'm sorry" wouldn't do. "What else did you hear?"

"Everything, enough."

"Why didn't you say something?"

"I spoke to you...when you came inside." She kept her back to him. "I asked you why you married me and you couldn't tell me. I asked you if you ever loved me. Remember?"

God, he remembered that. He remembered looking at her and knowing that he wanted her but having no idea how to respond to her questions. "Was that a test and I failed?"

"No, I just wanted the truth and you gave it to me."

"If I remember right, I didn't say anything."

"Exactly," she said turning to face him. "You didn't have anything to say."

"Sam, what did you want me to say? I cared about you and I married you. I wasn't some poor stupid pawn in all of it, but that didn't mean it was right. That didn't mean that I could make you happy. I never even thought I'd ever get married, then there we were. You deserved better than that.''

"I deserved a husband," she said tightly. "I got an affair that masqueraded as a marriage. And it's over. You're right, it's over. Live and learn. Sleep with someone, but don't marry them. Isn't that the lesson in this?"

"Sam, stop it," he said in a low voice, hating the bitterness that was in her words.

"Well, that would have made everything cheap, not complicated, but cheap," she said, and he saw the paleness coming back. "And then again, there wouldn't have been a divorce and all that inconvenience for both of us, either."

He took a step toward her, but he didn't reach out for her. He just stood there, stunned by his stupid idea that he could come here and find any peace, any closure. "Sam, don't do this."

"Don't do what? Speak the truth?" She shook her head, stopping immediately and taking in a soft breath.

"The truth is we're divorced." He spoke bluntly. "The truth is you've got your life and I've got mine. The truth is we had our time and it's over."

Sam's relief over Nick's not remembering their night together dissolved as she understood something else. Despite the fact that he'd never loved her, she'd loved him desperately. And their relationship was over. "Yes, I guess that's true," she said.

He leaned slightly forward. "So, I guess this is goodbye and good luck. I hope you find every happiness."

So polite. So final. So civilized. The world started to shift again. "Thanks for bringing back the locket," she said, and was horrified when Nick began to float in front of her eyes. She blinked rapidly, but it didn't help at all. She felt her legs give way, and she grabbed for Nick again. "Oh, wow," she whispered, balling his shirtfront in her hands. "I...I...I'm sorry."

"Now will you let me help you?" he asked in a low, rough voice.

She hesitated, then knew she needed him if she wanted to reach the house without falling down. "Just get me inside, and I...I can take it from there."

Nick was relieved that he didn't have to force her to let him help her. He put his arm around her shoulders, struck by her slenderness, ignoring the way she seemed to fit against him perfectly. Slowly they walked to the cottage. He barely noticed the flowers at the base of the veranda or the way the stairs squeaked under their weight as they made their way toward the front door.

He grasped the brass latch, and pushed the door open, entering a small foyer with faded cabbage-rose wallpaper. They turned right off the foyer into a parlor filled with wicker furniture. The room's leaded windows overlooked the veranda and the ocean.

They neared a couch and Sam let go of him to sink onto its blue plaid cushions. Nick stood over her as she eased back with a sigh.

"I'm calling a doctor," he told her.

"No, I don't need a doctor," she said, and he could see color coming back into her cheeks.

"You're sick."

"No, no, not sick. I just…I guess I forgot to eat and my blood sugar…I just need to sit for a while, then I'll get something to eat."

He looked through an open archway into another room at the front of the cottage. It was her studio. Paintings were propped against bare walls and her easel was positioned by the windows for the light. He could even catch the scent of paint and thinner in the air. A door at the back of the parlor opened into the kitchen.

"Okay, then, how about some tea, that peppermint tea you used to like?"

She was very still when he glanced at her, and her eyes were overly bright. "No, thanks. I'll be okay. Please, you can go."

She didn't look okay at all. "What do you want to eat?" he asked, not about to just walk out and leave her like this.

"I don't want you to…" She bit her lip. "I could use some water."

"Water and food," he said, then reached for her hand. She jerked at the contact, but let him lift her hand and turn it over. "Open up."

She opened her hand palm up, a palm touched by yellow paint. "What's the matter?"

"What were you painting?"

"What?" she asked, drawing her hand back into her lap.

"You have paint on your hand."

She looked down at her yellow-streaked palm, then said, "Hair. A child's hair, that blond color that flashes with sunlight."

That was too artistic for him, especially when he thought that the color could have been hers when the sunlight caught it just right. He didn't comment but headed toward the kitchen. He was at the kitchen door, ready to step into the very large room, when Sam's voice stopped him.

"Peanut butter," she called after him.

He turned, touching the door frame with one hand. "Excuse me?"

"Peanut butter. I'd like some peanut butter, please, and an apple."

"A sandwich and an apple?"

"No, just the jar of peanut butter and an apple cut up in wedges. The peanut butter's on the counter by the sink and there's an apple in the bowl on the table.''

"Okay," he said and walked into the kitchen. He found a knife in the dish rack by the sink, along with a plate. After cutting the apple into wedges, he opened the jar of peanut butter and noticed that the large container was already half-empty. "Do you need a spoon?" he called to her.

"No, that's okay," she replied. He was just about to reach for the plate with the apple on it when he noticed something on the window ledge over the sink. The bottle was almost lost among some seashells she'd obviously collected off the beach, but its bright pink cap stood out starkly against the shells.

One word on the label caught his attention. *Prenatal.* Setting the peanut butter jar down, he grabbed the bottle and read the label. Prenatal Vitamins. Prenatal? Sam?

He turned to find her standing at the kitchen door. This time, her dress wasn't billowing in the wind, the skirt no longer a shield from the truth. A truth that almost made him sick from shock. He saw the softly rounded shape of her stomach.

Sam was pregnant.

Why had he never even thought of another man in Sam's life? God, she was lovely, sexy, desirable. She wasn't meant to be alone. Hadn't she told him what she'd always dreamed of when she'd been in foster care—her own home, her own children. Everything he'd always thought as unnecessary in his life.

Now she'd realized her dream. And he'd been so involved in his own reactions to Sam, so confused about them, that he hadn't noticed. He couldn't stop staring at her.

He began to think she must have been pregnant when they'd met at Danforth's offices. For the first time in his life, he didn't have any words, so he turned away from the sight of Sam.

He stared blindly out the window and realized that she was probably living here with the father of the child. God knew how long she might have been with the man. He heard her move behind him, reach for the peanut butter jar and take a seat at the kitchen table.

When he glanced toward her, he found her sitting and dipping a slice of apple into the peanut butter. Thankfully, his emotions were settling down. He could feel the shock starting to filter out of him. Sam had her life. The life she'd wanted—just not with him.

"Are you feeling better?" he asked.

"Yes, thanks."

"You..." He couldn't take his eyes off her as she scooped more peanut butter with an apple wedge. "Where is he?"

Her hand jerked at his question and she paused

with the apple partway to her mouth. "Excuse me?"

"Your husband. Where is he?"

She set the peanut butter jar onto the table with a soft thud, then stared hard at the piece of apple in her hand. "Husband?"

"Never mind. I doubt that he'd want to meet me." Nick sure as hell didn't want to meet him. He just wanted out of here. "I better get going. Got a full day tomorrow. I just wanted to return the locket to you."

She automatically touched the locket she'd put back on, then looked at him, spots of high color on her cheeks. "Busy as usual," she said in a low voice.

As if proving her point, his cell phone rang. "Yes?"

"Nick? It's Greg."

He turned from Sam when he saw her touch her stomach, letting her hand settle on the filmy fabric that clung to her belly. "What is it?" he asked, leaning against the door frame and closing his eyes.

"The deposition might be back on for tomorrow. At least they're hinting that it could happen. They need those revised questions and they want full approval. I told them I'd speak with you, see what you thought."

He could barely focus on work at that moment. "What do you think?"

Greg paused, obviously not used to Nick hesitating in any way. "Why not? Let them get approval and go with whatever you can get out of them. What's to lose? What do you think?"

"Sounds fine to me."

"Okay, stay put and work on the revisions. Meanwhile, I'll get hold of them, find out anything else I can and tell them we'll be in touch tomorrow. How's that?"

"You're earning your big bucks," Nick said. "Be in touch."

He flipped the phone shut and took a breath, bracing himself to turn and say goodbye to Sam. But she wasn't there when he turned. He hadn't heard her move, although the door to the back porch was open. A slight breeze was trickling into the kitchen and the sounds of birds echoed slightly in the stillness.

Nick crossed the room and stepped through the open door onto the wraparound porch. Sam was sitting on the top step. Her legs were drawn up to her middle, her arms around them, her head pressed to her knees.

"That was Greg," he said.

"Things to do, people to meet?" she asked, her voice muffled.

"Well, things to do, that's for sure."

She lifted her head to look at his car parked by the back steps. "Always things to do. Nothing's changed, has it?"

"I wouldn't say that," he murmured.

"I guess not," she said in a voice so low he almost didn't hear.

He knew he should leave, but he couldn't until he said something. Moving closer, Nick stopped just behind her. "So, you're pregnant?" The question sounded so incredibly stupid to his own ears. Of course she was pregnant. If the breeze hadn't been billowing her loose dress around her before, he would have noticed that fact right away.

She let out a deep sigh and nodded. "Yes."

"Why didn't you tell me that you were pregnant when we were at Danforth's?"

Sam stared out at the horizon, the stinging in her eyes uncomfortable, but nothing compared to having Nick this close. She'd been so stunned by his question about a husband and in turmoil over how to tell him about the child.

*"Nick, I'm having your baby."* That sounded direct and right, but something inside her wouldn't let her say the words.

She'd come out here to think, but that hadn't helped. She had to tell him, yet she couldn't form the words. She'd practiced them enough, long into the empty nights. She'd rehearsed what to say, what not to say, what to do. But none of that mattered now. The reality was that she was scared to death. Her heart was pounding and her stomach was in knots. Nothing was ever simple with Nick.

He thought she'd fallen into bed with someone else, that she'd been pregnant when she saw him the last time and kept it from him. From the moment she knew she was carrying his child, Sam had accepted she'd tell Nick. How could she not tell him that he had a child? She'd thought he wouldn't be happy, that he really would just see it as a nuisance more than anything. Maybe he'd offer support, the right thing to do under the circumstances, but she'd decided she wasn't going to take it. Still, she had never imagined he'd jump to the conclusion that she was carrying another man's child.

But why wouldn't he? He didn't remember what had happened that night. They hadn't been together—at least as far as he knew—for almost a year. No, he'd rather think that she'd been with another man, got pregnant and that was it. And that hurt.

"Sam, how could you have stood there and not told me or Danforth what was going on?"

"I wasn't…" She didn't know what to say, what not to say.

"It just seems if someone you're divorcing is pregnant with your child…" His words died away, and she was thankful she wasn't looking at him, not when he said, "Thank God that wasn't the case."

"What would you have done if it had been yours?" she asked in a small voice.

She heard his rough exhale of air. "It wasn't, so that's not relevant."

"Not relevant," she echoed, then gripped the porch support and stood. The world was still far from steady, but she was fine if she held on to the post and kept her eyes closed.

"Where's your husband?"

His words rocked her world again. She pressed one hand to her middle. Husband. God, the word made her ache. "I don't…" She found herself unable to finish when she opened her eyes and found the world undulating in front of her. A fear started to seep into her. If there was anything wrong with the baby… "I…I'll just go inside, and you can leave, meet your people and do whatever it is you have to do."

Nick didn't move. His eyes narrowed on her, the hazel color darkening. "Where in the hell is your husband?"

## Chapter Eight

Where was her "husband?" Nick wanted to know. Samantha only had one word in reply. "Gone," she said. And it was so true.

At her response, Nick moved closer, studying her intently and making it physically impossible for her to get past him and into the house. "You're still not okay, and I'm calling your doctor," he said.

"No, please, I can call, and—"

"I'm calling," he said abruptly. "What's his name and number?"

She tried to steady her world, but the dizziness continued and she was starting to get scared. "Dr. Barnet. His...his number is by the kitchen phone."

He motioned her to the step. "Sit down, and I'll be right back."

Then he was gone and she did as he said. She could hear Nick moving around in the kitchen, then his muffled voice as he spoke on the phone.

She heard Nick come back out on the porch and knew he was standing behind her. "The doctor wants to talk to you," he said.

Easing herself to her feet, Sam turned and accepted Nick's hand for support. His fingers closed around hers, and she let him help her back into the house. She sank onto a kitchen chair and Nick handed her the receiver. But he didn't move away while she pressed it to her ear.

"Dr. Barnet?"

"You're having problems, Samantha?"

"I'm feeling very light-headed, a little unsteady."

"Any pain?"

"No."

"Any spotting?"

"No, nothing, just a fuzzy head."

"How about food? When's the last meal you had?"

"I just had some peanut butter and an apple. But I didn't have any breakfast."

"Okay, you get some more to eat, keep your feet up and rest, and call again if you need me. If not, come by tomorrow. Let's see..." He was silent for a minute, then said, "I'm tied up most of the day with a cesarean, but..." He exhaled. "It looks as if I can see you around four. I can check on things then."

"Okay, thanks," she said, and held the phone out to Nick.

He took it, then spoke into the receiver. "What do you think?" Nick listened, nodded, then said, "Okay, that's doable. Tomorrow at four. She'll be there. Thank you." He turned to Sam. "The doctor says you need to eat more, you have to take it easy, and he wants to see you tomorrow," Nick told her after he hung up the phone.

"I know," she said.

"Where's your bedroom?"

She peered up at him. "What?"

"He said for you to rest."

"Nick, no, you don't have to—"

"No, I don't, but I am."

"I'm not an invalid." She got to her feet, the light-headedness receding slightly. She gripped the back of the chair, steadied herself, then looked at Nick. "See, I'm okay." He kept silent as she experimented with letting go of her support, then carefully walked toward the front of the house.

Without warning, her knees buckled, and before she could catch herself, Nick had her. She was being lifted into his arms, the beating of his heart against the flat of her palm pressed to his chest. "Sure you're okay," he muttered.

"Just put me down," she insisted, but didn't have the strength to make him do her bidding.

Nick didn't pay any attention to her anyway but asked again, "Where's your bedroom?"

"Upstairs."

He carried her to the stairs and up to the second floor. She closed her eyes tightly, memories of Nick carrying her up from the beach in Malibu so clear that the past months might never have been.

"I guess I don't have to ask which room," he said, his voice rumbling against her cheek.

She opened her eyes, and they were in the *only* room at the top of the stairs. Her bedroom ran the length of the house. There were dormer windows on both sides, with her brass bed positioned in front of the windows that overlooked the ocean. The hardwood floors creaked with each step Nick took.

Shadows were starting to gather outside as Nick carried her over to the bed. He eased her down on top of the pale blue comforter and into the bank of pillows, then stood slightly over her.

"Food. The doctor said you had to eat some more, so what will it be?"

"The peanut butter and the rest of the apple," she said. With a nod, he turned and went back down the stairs.

Sam watched until he was gone, then she reached for the phone on her nightstand. Quickly, she called Mrs. Douglas but only reached the elderly woman's answering machine. "Please just leave a message and I will return your call.'' Sam had thought if Mrs. Douglas was nearby, Nick would leave without argument. But that wasn't going to work out.

She sank back into the pillows, one hand over her eyes, the other protectively resting on her stomach. She tried to breathe slowly, evenly, and if she tried really hard, she knew she could make believe that Nick's being here was all a dream.

A dream. Tomorrow she would wake up and find he had never been here. She'd be in control. And she'd contact Nick later, much later, about the baby. She exhaled, stretched her legs out and turned on her side, facing the far wall. This was only a dream like her other dreams.

Memories assailed her. She could still hear Nick saying, ''If that's what you want, Samantha, we'll get married. I know a judge, and he won't give us a hard time. In an hour we can be married.''

And adding, ''I've never wanted anyone like I want you.''

Nick holding her, slipping a simple solitaire on her finger. Nick kissing her, then they were making love for the first time.

Friends had told her the first time would be a disappointment, that she'd regret waiting till her wedding night, but they'd been so wrong. It had been explosive, almost painful, but a fulfillment she'd never even suspected existed. Nick over her,

Nick inside her. Nick. His breathing almost her own breathing. The moans of pleasure, his words just for her, words— "Sam?"

That voice wasn't from the past, but now. Here. Beside her. She fluttered her eyes open, twisted a bit, and saw Nick setting a tray on the nightstand.

"A peanut butter sandwich and more peanut butter, and an apple and some milk," he said, pointing to the tray.

She pushed herself up to a sitting position, brushing at her tangled hair. "Thanks," she said as she took the plate from Nick's hand, thankful he hadn't turned on the light. The shadows were much kinder, a place where she didn't have to focus too clearly on Nick's face. She picked up a piece of apple, scooped up some peanut butter and nibbled on it.

"I haven't had peanut butter since I was in military school, then I think it was punishment for something. I can't remember." He sat down on the edge of the bed as if it was the most natural thing in the world to do. "I seem to remember hating it but liking bologna. Can't stand bologna today."

"I never knew you went to military school," she said, tearing a sandwich half in two.

"I never knew you ran away a lot. Lots of things we don't know about each other, aren't there?" He motioned to the sandwich in her hand. "Eat. I'll talk." When she took a bite, he said, "Military school wasn't one of my finest hours. I think it was during the three years of my mother's fourth marriage, or maybe it was the four years of her third marriage. It's hard to keep track.''

She'd never met his parents and doubted that they knew anything about her. ''How many times was your mother married?''

He frowned slightly. ''Five times, I think. I haven't had any contact with her for the past several years so she could have had a couple more husbands by now. It's hard to say.''

''I had no idea,'' she breathed.

''Now my father, he's a bit more conservative. Married just three times. But I believe his last wife, my stepmother, is about thirty years younger than him and running him ragged.''

''Do you see him very much?''

He shook his head. ''Not if I can help it.''

She couldn't imagine having parents and never seeing them, and that brought her own dilemma back to her full force. She also couldn't imagine her child never knowing his or her father, but right now she wondered if Nick would even want to see a child of his. ''That's sad,'' she said as she shifted and put the plate on the tray, then picked up the glass of milk. ''Don't you ever wish you had a real mother and father?''

He chuckled roughly but not with much humor. ''Oh, my parents are real enough, too real. And no,

I never wanted Ozzie and Harriet, if that's what you mean."

She didn't really know what she meant by a real mother and father because she'd never had them. But that's what she wanted for her child. Another dream. She sipped some cool milk, then rested the glass on her thigh. "I guess that's it. I don't know. But it seems sad to have a mother and father and never see them or be with them." The room had dimmed until Nick was just a shape beside her on the bed. And the gathering darkness let her say things she'd never said to anyone before. "My parents were gone before I knew what a mother or father meant."

"You never talked about that to me. And I hated to ask."

"It's okay. I mean, I don't remember any of what happened." She touched the locket at her throat. "A social worker told me that the files said they were killed when I was a year and a half old. That's when I went into foster care. I couldn't be adopted because they were looking for relatives, and by the time they found out there wasn't anyone, I was considered too old for adoption."

"I had no idea," he said. "How old you were when you stayed here?"

"Twelve. The family was okay. Nice enough, I guess, but they had kids of their own, and I was odd man out. I'd run away, come here and sit outside looking at the cottage. I never wanted the big house, just this place. It looked magical to me." She took a quick sip. "That's enough of that," she murmured, and drank the last of her milk.

He silently took the glass from her and put it on the tray. She heard a snap as he turned on the small table lamp. Its weak glow barely lit the room, but she could see Nick move to sit back on the bed, resting against the brass rails at the foot. He crossed his arms over his chest and she heard him exhale. "We never did talk very much, did we, Sam?"

The words conjured up so much of what their life had been together, and that was underscored by the fact that he was sitting on her bed. She felt heat flood her face.

"We never talked about your parents, that's for sure. Or about my parents, or about what either one of us wanted for the future." She smoothed the fine material of her dress. "Big mistake, huh?"

"Very big mistake." He stood and walked to a window, staring out at the early evening sky. "But it's done, and we both escaped without too much damage. And a lesson is learned."

"What lesson?"

He turned. "I learned just how good I am at marriage. I always suspected that it was wrong for me, but I had to experience it to realize how miserable I am at it. It must be in my genes."

"What about children?" she asked, surprising herself by the question.

"Children?" He snorted derisively. "I'd be a disaster with kids. No, you have them and let me know all about it, but it's not something I'm ever going to want."

Sam could feel her heart sinking with each word he uttered. It was the reaction she had expected, but to hear him say it seemed to make it all the more devastating.

"Do you really mean that?" she asked, barely able to speak the works loudly enough for him to hear, her throat tight with tears.

"Mean what?"

"That…you don't ever want children?" she asked, and could hear a sob in her voice. God, she was going to cry. She didn't want to do that, but her hormones were totally out of control.

"I'd never inflict myself on any kid," he said. "No, as far as I'm concerned, others can procreate and I'll sit by and let them. You and your husband go for it, and good luck to you."

The tears that had been so close to the surface came then, spilling onto her cheeks. She took a gulping breath but couldn't stop the sobs and blindly felt for the box of tissues on the nightstand.

"Hey, sorry, I didn't mean to make you cry," Nick said, crouching beside her to hand her a tissue. "I was just telling you how I felt. It doesn't matter. It's not important."

"It…it is important," she sobbed. "It's really important."

"Sam, it's not. It's a moot point with me. You, on the other hand, have passed the surmising state and are well into the realm of parenthood." That made her sob more loudly, and Nick moved even closer. "Hey, please, no, don't do this." She'd never cried in front of him, not even during their final argument. Her tears had been saved for the time she was completely alone. But she couldn't stop them. When he touched her, brushing her hair back from her cheeks, she jerked away.

"No, don't," she gasped, swiping at her face with the crumpled tissue. "I'm sorry. It's…it's being pregnant. It just…makes me so emotional, and things are all mixed up and…" She took a gulping breath and swallowed hard. "I'm sorry. First I'm almost fainting and now I'm crying. I don't do this. I mean, I never, hardly ever do this."

"It's okay," he said.

"Damn it," she muttered, sitting back, "it's not okay. It's terrible and it's wrong."

"It's just emotions."

"Yeah sure," she breathed, thankful that the tears were stopping. She wiped her eyes with the tissue, then sank onto a pillow with a sigh. "I'm okay, really. I'm okay. And you can go now." She sniffed softly. "I know you've got work to do. Thanks for everything."

Nick had never done well with emotions, not with his own or with anyone else's. Even when Sam had walked out, she'd done it quietly. She'd told him she couldn't stay, that the marriage was a mistake and she was leaving. She hadn't cried or raged or screamed. She'd just left and moved here.

He wondered if she'd already known the man she would eventually marry next. If the guy she'd found was already in the picture and the reason she'd given up on *their* marriage so easily. That possibility tore at him almost as much as the sudden thought that he was in "their room" and sitting on "their bed." He'd never been jealous, ever. He'd never come close, but at that moment he knew a jealousy that was completely encompassing. And unsettling.

He moved away from the bed and from the idea of Samantha sleeping with another man, a man who touched her and made love to her. It was more than he wanted to think about. And when she touched her stomach, the visible result of that love-making, he spoke quickly. "You feel better? You think you'll be okay?"

"Sure, I'm lots better. The peanut butter really helped."

"Tomorrow at four you'll see your doctor?"

"Of course."

He glanced around the shadowy room. "You'll have someone here with you soon, won't you?"

She didn't speak, and when he looked back at her, she was sitting very still, one hand splayed on her stomach, the other fiddling with the locket.

"Sam?"

"Uh, probably not."

"What about your husband? Won't he be back soon?" Nick asked, hoping he'd be gone before the other man returned.

"He's…Nick, he…you don't—"

"What? Is he working?" He knew he was driven by work, but if Sam needed him… He stopped that thought. He had no right to be angry with some guy he'd never even met. "Can I ask you something?"

She nodded.

"How did this happen?"

"What?"

He gripped the brass rail at the foot of the bed, and found he had to clear his throat before he could get out the question that had plagued him since he'd discovered her condition. "How did you get pregnant?"

That brought a slight chuckle from her, an unsteady, forced sound. "Do I really need to explain?"

"I mean, how did you let it happen?"

"I didn't *let* it happen. It wasn't planned. I was

as shocked as you probably were. Maybe more so.''

He very much doubted she was more surprised than he had been at the moment he realized she was pregnant. The light barely touched her, its soft glow revealing a slight frown on her face, but her eyes were lost to him.

As he looked at her in the bed, at her breathtaking beauty, a thought hit him in his gut. Sam wouldn't sleep with him until he'd married her. She'd been a virgin, something he never would have suspected of someone as beautiful as her. But she sure as hell had slept with the baby's father before they'd gotten married.

"Were we still married when you slept with him? That's what I'm talking about. We got married first. But with this guy—"

She cut him off. "This guy?" she echoed. Her eyes were wide and unblinking.

"The baby's father. I want to know if you went against everything you ever told me you valued."

She shrugged, a fluttery, vulnerable motion that shook him to his core almost as much as the words she uttered in little more than a whisper. "I loved him."

That wasn't what he wanted to hear at all; he knew that as soon as the words hung between them. He'd never fully understood the concept of love or even wanted to. His parents had supposedly loved each other, but after promising "till death us do part," the death of their love had occurred rather quickly.

Love? He didn't believe in it, never had. He'd never felt it or seen it. What he felt for Sam, or what he used to feel for her, probably came as close to love as anything ever had in his life. But when she'd asked him about loving her, he couldn't lie to her. He hadn't said a word. And she'd left. Now she was telling him that she loved the baby's father.

"That's all it took?" he asked roughly. There was an edge to his voice that he hated but couldn't stop, not even when he saw her flinch and wrap her arms around herself. "Thinking you loved him?"

"You don't understand, do you?" she whispered.

No, he didn't understand. Why was he torturing himself over something that was nothing to him anymore? Surely the dreams would stop now. They'd been burned out by this anger and stupid jealousy. He wanted this conversation over even though he'd started it himself. "Do you need anything else?" he asked as he moved to leave the room.

"No."

A single word that sounded so horribly final.

"Okay. Now what's Mrs. Douglas's phone number?"

"Why?"

"I'll call her, see if she can stay here with you for the night. The doctor said you shouldn't be left alone, and since she's the only one around, I thought that would be a solution."

"No," she said, getting off the bed. "Don't do that. She's sweet, but she's also…well, she's gone out for the night. But thanks for caring."

He looked down at her. Hell, yes, he cared. He would always care about her. And that's the only reason he found himself saying, "Okay, if she's not available, I am. I'll use the couch in the parlor."

"Oh, no, you won't."

"Oh, yes, I will. I've got work to do, and by the time I drive all the way back to San Francisco and find a hotel, it'll be really late. I take it you've got a phone jack down there somewhere."

"Nick, please, you can't—"

"Yes, I can. Since your husband chooses to be away, I'm staying until he shows up, or Mrs. Douglas shows up, or the doctor says you're okay. And as for your driving yourself into town to see the doctor tomorrow, well, unless you want to play martyr, I'd say you should welcome a ride from someone."

"Go away, Nick," she muttered.

"Good night, Samantha," he said, then motioned to the remaining food. "Eat some more. You'll feel better." Then he left. He was committed now, he realized. He'd have to stay until he could get ahold of Mrs. Douglas or until someone was here for Sam.

Not smart, he thought as he went down the stairs and into the parlor. Not smart at all. But he wasn't leaving, not just yet.

# Chapter Nine

Sam couldn't think straight. All she had to do was open her mouth and tell Nick the baby was his, and he'd leave. But she couldn't make herself do it now, not after what he'd said about children. The time was wrong. This was the wrong place. And she was in the wrong emotional state to tell him. The last thing she wanted to do was cry in front of him again. No, now wasn't the time. But she'd do it soon.

She crossed to the bathroom and stripped off her clothes, then reached for a pale pink cotton nightgown hanging on the back of the door.

She hesitated when she caught a glimpse of herself in the mottled mirror over the sink. She looked pale, her eyes shadowed and a bit red-rimmed from crying. Her hair was a mess, and whatever makeup she might have had on at one time had completely disappeared. She grimaced at her reflection, then glanced down and saw the gentle swell of her stomach.

It was real. So real. She touched her bare belly, slowly rubbing her hand in circles as she said softly, "It's just you and me, kiddo." Her throat tightened, and she grabbed the gown and slipped it over her head.

Back in the bedroom, she tugged back the comforter and accidentally caught the food-laden tray with the edge, sending it flying to the floor with a crash. The peanut butter jar rolled across the hardwood floor and the pieces of apple flew everywhere. The plate broke neatly in half. The empty glass somehow escaped undamaged.

With a muttered oath of frustration, she bent to pick up the mess. She was reaching for the peanut butter jar that had almost rolled under the bed when she heard Nick call out, "Sam? What's wrong?" He burst into the bedroom, wearing only his jeans. "Are you all right?" he demanded as he came toward her.

She held up the jar. "I knocked the tray off the nightstand. Sorry."

"Are you having another dizzy spell again?" he asked.

"No, I'm not. It was just a silly accident and…" When she watched him stoop to the floor, her mouth literally went dry at the sight of his bare back as he picked up the apple pieces. She'd always loved his broad, square shoulders and his smooth, strong-looking back. He dropped the fruit on the nightstand and turned. If she thought the sight of his naked back was wreaking havoc with her senses, seeing his naked chest made her heart hammer.

It was just like the first time, seeing his tanned skin in the low light, the muscles, a suggestion of dark hair running over his flat stomach to disappear into the waistband of his jeans. She felt like a fifteen-year-old, all flustered and weak in the knees. And it wasn't from lack of food or being pregnant this time. It was pure lust.

"I thought you'd fallen or something," Nick said, approaching her again.

Unable to continue looking at him, she reached for the brass rail of the bed and had to make herself take a breath. "I'm sorry. I...I wasn't watching and everything fell." She turned back to Nick but misjudged how close he was and ran right into him. All muscles and hardness, male scent and slick heat. It was overwhelming.

He had her by her shoulders, both hands supporting her, and she couldn't stop the instinctive twisting of an escape attempt. Or hitting the foot of the bed with her hip and throwing herself off balance the other way. Nick had her again, holding on to her, steadying her, only inches from her, his hands on her upper arms now.

She forced herself to stop, not to panic at his touch, even though her heart beat rapidly and her chest tightened to the point where she almost felt sick. "Nick, don't," she managed to mutter.

"Don't what?" he asked, his voice low and rough.

She trembled as she looked up at him, into intense eyes that robbed her of any sense of space or time. His grip on her eased, almost releasing her, but not quite. His fingers still circled her upper arms, but they moved slowly up and down her skin, and her trembling increased.

"Oh, Nick," she whispered.

"Sam, I don't understand any of this." His hands shifted up over her shoulders to her throat until they were gently framing her face. His thumbs made slow, hypnotic circles on her cheeks. "I wish you'd never heard Greg and me, but I still don't understand why you left. Why you had to go."

She couldn't get any words out. If she talked, she knew she'd start crying. She didn't understand anything anymore, either; not how she could know so clearly that she had to be away from Nick, yet wanting nothing more than to fall into his arms and stay there forever. "You...you..." She took an unsteady breath, then managed, "It was wrong, too...too fast. It was a mistake."

"Why couldn't we have just let it run its

course?'' he breathed, his touch on her stilling. ''God, I've wanted you forever. That never stopped.''

It hadn't for her, either. ''I know, I know. It's just not right.''

Without warning, he leaned toward her, brushing his lips lightly over hers before she understood what he intended to do. Then he was gazing down at her again. ''It's there, isn't it? It's still all there.''

She touched her tongue to her lips, taking his taste into her mouth. ''What?''

''You and me. It never stopped. It never could.'' He was closer now, so close that his breath brushed her skin with heat. ''Damn it, I want you. I've had these dreams that never stop—dreams of you and me. I never stopped wanting you or needing you.''

She waited, her heart hammering in her chest. For a moment, for a shining second, she thought he was going to say that he'd always loved her, that he loved her now. But he never said that. Instead, he kissed her again, but not with a light or fleeting touch this time.

The contact was hot and demanding. His tongue invaded her mouth as her lips parted and she let him inside her, touching her soul. His arms were around her, pressing her to him, and for an instant she felt his heart beating against hers through the thin cotton of her nightgown. A raw hunger began growing inside her that was terrifying.

She held on to him, pressing against him, trying to dissolve into him. If they were one, she wouldn't have to let go; she wouldn't have to be alone again. Nick was there, and she loved him with a passion that defied logic or understanding. Then Nick lifted her up and onto the bed so that she was almost at eye level with him.

His hazel eyes burned into hers, never straying as his hands reached for the straps of her nightgown and slowly slipped them off her shoulders. She felt every sensation of the material slipping lower on her arms, of her bare skin being exposed to the air and to Nick's gaze. The soft material bunched at her hips and waist, and her breasts swelled at the exposure.

Her nipples hardened; she felt the tightening even before Nick touched her. They were so sensitive that when his fingers actually made contact, they almost ached. They tightened even more when he bent low and found one nipple with his lips. The sensation was so intense, she almost cried as the feelings coursed through her, intensifying, clenching at her heart.

She loved him and needed him, and she instinctively wanted to be closer, to feel skin against skin. She circled his neck with her arms and drew him even closer, falling back onto the bed with him, finding his mouth with hers, kissing him with a hunger that had a life of its own. She pressed her breasts to his chest, kissing his bare shoulder, moaning from a desire that overwhelmed her.

She felt every inch of his body against hers, felt his need for her growing hard against her. Breast to chest, stomach to stomach, hips against hips, and she knew that she was home. She was in the place that only he could share with her, that refuge in the world that she had always been looking for. Nick. Here. With her. She twisted, tasting his skin with her tongue, feeling his heart beat against her lips. She touched his nipple, hard and sensitive when her lips found it, and a low, rumbling moan came from him.

Then he was kissing her, and she knew that all she wanted in this world was to make love with him again. To lie with him, feel him surrounding her, to have that moment where she felt complete and whole again, where she felt alive.

She strained against him, and at that moment her world stopped. It was the baby. She felt it—a soft blip as her stomach pressed against Nick. A kick that was so slight, yet so monumental. She gasped, drawing back, and it happened again. The baby. She'd felt connected to it ever since knowing it existed, but in that moment, she felt its reality.

She splayed her fingers over her stomach, willing that sensation again. Her other hand was pressed to Nick's heart, an invisible connection between the three of them. A spiritual connection that filled her soul with wonder and awe.

"What is it? Did I hurt you?" Nick asked.

She met his gaze, her love for him as complete and uncompromising as her new love for their child. "The...the baby, I felt it move," she whispered, still in awe.

Nick shook his head. "Oh, God." He grimaced, then pushed back abruptly, putting distance between them. She didn't have to look into his eyes to know what she'd see. Kissing and touching were one thing, but knowing that a child was there between them was more than he could deal with. Lust was lust. It never was love.

Nick moved off the bed, leaving a cold, barren space behind him. Standing at the bedside, looking down at her, he pushed his hands into his pockets, further exposing the hard need that only his jeans contained. Embarrassed by her nakedness, Samantha twisted in the opposite direction, tugging at her nightgown as she sat up on the far side of the bed.

She pulled the soft cotton over her aching breasts and tugged the straps back over her shoulders.

"Good night," Nick said in a low whisper. Then she heard him walk across the floor and take the steps quickly to get away.

Her whole body ached with frustration, yet as she touched her stomach and felt that stirring again, she knew something was very right. One thing in her life was perfect. Even when Nick had gone, never to be a part of her life again, she'd have the child. She'd have part of him.

NICK FELT AS IF he had been jerked out of one of his dreams again—a dream of fire and silk and passion—to be thrown into a reality he couldn't begin to comprehend at that moment. He literally ached with need for the woman on the bed upstairs, but this time his ache wasn't caused by a dream.

He went into the kitchen and tried to call Mrs. Douglas, but he only got the answering machine. He hung up without leaving a message and walked outside, down onto the lawn. Damn it, nothing was right. He ran a hand roughly over his face as his bare feet pressed into the thick grass on his way to the bluffs. There was no way he could stay in the house right then. Needing air and space, he headed down the path and across the sand to the shoreline.

In the darkness, he stripped off the last of his clothes, then waded naked into the lapping waves. When he was waist-deep, he dived below the surface and glided in nothingness for as long as he could hold his breath. Only when he felt as if his lungs would burst did he surface into the air. The full moon overhead provided the only light and he flipped onto his back, letting himself float.

As he lay suspended between heaven and earth, Nick recalled the night Sam had left him. She'd been dressed in some drab pair of slacks and a loose white blouse, carrying two bags.

"What's going on?" he'd asked, but knew the answer before she gave it.

"I'm leaving." Simple words. Understandable words.

He could still remember how that night's sky had appeared. A sliver of a moon, the stars.

"I left you a letter," she'd said softly, her voice husky. "This was all a mistake, a terrible mistake. Neither one of us should have gotten married. Stupid, really."

When he'd tried to go closer to her, she'd retreated even more. "Don't. Let's just get this over with. You're not into marriage, and I'm not into this." She motioned vaguely with her head to the room. "I was wrong. I admit it. It's better if I just go."

He couldn't remember now what he'd felt. Relief? Anger? He didn't know. "Where are you going?"

"I don't know yet, but away from here, away from Los Angeles."

He'd argued with her, he knew that, but he didn't recall what his argument had been because deep down inside, he'd been relieved. There was no mess, no fuss, just the goodbye. Maybe she'd said she was "very sure". He floated on the water, memories blurred at first, then gradually coming into focus. He did remember the goodbye, the awkward moment when he'd moved aside and let her leave. The way the door sounded when she closed it behind her. Yes, he remembered that, the echo in the emptiness.

Nick flipped over on his stomach and stroked toward shore. He remembered the first night in his bed without her, that sense of losing something he'd never really had. He'd told himself it was for the best, that she'd saved them both misery, but he realized now that was a lie.

He still felt miserable. Even so, that didn't make their reasons for divorcing any different. Sam still wanted what he didn't. She was a stranger he barely knew. A stranger he could want with a white-hot passion, but a stranger he still didn't understand. Nick felt the sand under his feet, stood and waded out of the water onto the shore. He stopped just long enough to scoop up his clothes, then started up the bluff.

Once on the grass, he stopped to look at the cottage, awash in the moonlight. As he pulled on his jeans, Nick noticed Sam's bedroom window was dark; the only lights on were those in the kitchen. In such a setting, the cottage looked enchanted, just as Sam had said. A fairy tale. He hadn't believed in fairy tales for years…if ever.

And he wasn't going to start thinking up fairy tales now about himself and a married woman who was going to have another man's child.

"Mr. Viera?"

The voice of Mrs. Douglas as she emerged from the shadows startled him, and he turned, not sure just how long she'd been there. "Hello, Mrs. Douglas."

The light from the moon outlined her form as she moved forward. "I was out for a walk and thought I saw you coming up from the beach. I was surprised you were still here."

He wouldn't be for long, now that she'd returned. "I tried to call you earlier."

"Me? Did you think of an attorney who could settle that land problem for me?" As she came closer, he was a bit surprised to see that she was wearing running shoes with her dress.

"No, no, I haven't. It's not about that." He raked his fingers through his damp hair. "It's about Sam."

"Samantha? What about her?" She peered at him sharply. "Oh, I know what it is. You found out about the baby, didn't you?"

"Yes, but—"

"Mr. Viera, your ex-wife is a wonderful girl. She's just thrilled about the child, you know. And so am I. It's been a long time since tiny tots wandered around here." She sighed. "I think it will be lovely when the wee one comes, don't you?"

"Mrs. Douglas, Sam's been having dizzy spells."

"Oh, my, is she all right?"

"Yes, but the doctor wants to see her tomorrow at four. And he doesn't want her to be alone. I was calling to see if you could stay with her and maybe take her to the doctor's tomorrow."

"Oh, dear, yes, I see. But I can't do it. You see, I can't leave Owen alone, and I don't drive. But if you need chicken soup or some fresh fruit, just call. I'll get it over to you as quick as a wink."

"Maybe Sam could stay at your house?"

"I don't think so. She doesn't like Owen, and Owen, well, he's not fond of anyone being around except me. That wouldn't do. But, as I said, chicken soup and fruit. No problem. And since you're here, she's not alone, and I saw your car, so you drive." She patted his arm. "Everything works out for the best, don't you think?"

He didn't have a clue. "What about her husband?"

She studied him for a long moment, then shook her head. "Oh, dear, I don't think..." Her voice dropped to a whisper. "There is no husband. Not that I'm judging, but Samantha lives here alone."

Nick wasn't sure he'd heard right. "He doesn't live with her?"

"Dear, he doesn't exist," she said, and patted his arm again. "But you are here."

He stared at the elderly woman. Her face was so close to his but he saw the moon reflected in her bifocals. "He doesn't exist?"

She cocked her head to one side, then leaned toward him as if she was afraid of being overheard. "Dear, you didn't hear it from me, okay? Our little secret?"

Sam wasn't married? The father of the child wasn't with her? He felt as if he'd taken a blow to the stomach. "Are you sure about this?"

"Oh, yes, very sure. Samantha's told me things…well, that's private, but I can assure you that you are the only husband she's ever had." She cleared her throat. "And that is all I'm going to say. Now, I'm off for a walk. Then back to Owen. You take care of our Samantha, and if you need the soup, just call. As I said, everything works out just the way it's supposed to, don't you think?"

She disappeared into the darkness of the trees that rimmed the property. Nick stared after her for a long moment, then turned and headed toward the cottage. He was staying, at least until morning. He'd find out what was going on then—if Mrs. Douglas was telling the truth or if she was just plain crazy.

SLEEP WAS ELUDING SAM, as unattainable as peace was at that moment. She lay on her back, then turned on her side, pulled her legs up to her stomach and closed her eyes. The sound of the front door closing made her start slightly, then she heard Nick moving around downstairs. She closed her eyes so tightly that colors danced behind her lids. Then there was silence. Complete silence.

She shifted, stretching out on her back again and resting her hands on her stomach. Right then, the baby moved again—a fluttery feeling, a sensation so unique that it seemed almost surreal. Tears slipped from her eyes, silently running down her cheeks. A child conceived in love on her part. A child that she'd love forever, the way she loved its father.

She couldn't change her feelings for Nick, but she could make her own life and protect her child. That she could do. That she had control over. She swiped at the tears on her cheeks and made a vow that the baby would be safe and loved, no matter what.

NICK WENT INSIDE, took one look at the laptop that he'd brought in from the car and ignored it. He stretched out on the couch in the dimly lit parlor and closed his eyes. There were no sounds from upstairs, yet he could feel Sam's presence there. And the time when he could have gone up to her, gotten into bed with her and made love to her, taunted him.

He sat up, put his elbows on his knees and rested his head in his hands. God, he could almost taste her on his lips. He imagined her breasts—fuller than they'd been before—against his chest, recalled the need for her filling his body. And he remembered his jealousy of a man who might not exist.

Nick stood and looked around at the wicker and delicate fabrics. The braided rug on the floor, the silk flowers arranged on a breakfront. Sam's house. Her place. A place she was alone in. A woman's house without any touch of a man except what he'd brought with him. He quietly walked through the house, past her paintings lost in the shadows and into the kitchen. He turned on the light, squinted at the offending brightness, then glanced around.

He needed a drink, a strong drink. Opening several cupboards, he found the closest he could get to a real drink was a couple of small bottles that the airlines gave out—one of rum, one of brandy. There was little more than a mouthful in each, but he picked both bottles up, turned off the light and returned to the parlor.

Back on the couch, he turned out the last light and opened the rum. He drank it in two swallows, then reached for the other bottle. This really was a woman's home, he thought, a feminine home.

And there wasn't a trace of a man here, not even in the bathroom.

Stretching out, he stared above him into the shadows of the ceiling. There was no man. Mrs. Douglas was right. He took a ragged breath. Either he'd left right away, or he'd never been here.

Opening the other bottle, Nick downed it in one long gulp. As the fire spread in his middle, so did a sick feeling. Sam was pregnant. No matter how he tried to figure it out, the result was always the same. She'd either had another short marriage or she'd never married the father of her child. He swallowed hard at the sudden anger that tightened his throat.

She'd insisted on marrying him. She'd insisted on having the piece of paper. But with this other man, she hadn't been so particular. That thought sickened him. Then he recalled Sam saying, "I loved him," and he got to his feet again.

Out on the front porch, he sank onto the top step and stared out into the night, trying to make sense out of a life that had suddenly gone completely out of his control.

## Chapter Ten

Sam woke with a start, confused and disoriented for a moment, then she remembered everything. Nick. He'd gone. She'd heard him during the night, heard some sort of conversation on the phone and him moving around, and just before she'd fallen asleep, she'd thought she heard Nick leave.

The smell of bacon was in the air, mingling with the rich aroma of coffee and maybe toast. Mrs. Douglas must be here, she thought. Pushing herself up, she realized that the sun was fairly high in the sky. She took a deep breath, then got out of bed and headed for the bathroom. Nick had gone, and when she saw him again, it would be on her terms.

Quickly, she dressed in loose white shorts and a straight blue overshirt. Then, with her hair brushed back from her face and without makeup, she went downstairs in her bare feet.

She stepped into the studio, then saw movement in the kitchen. But it wasn't Mrs. Douglas. She saw

Nick at the sink. Nick in a plain short-sleeved white shirt and jeans, his feet bare as well. Swallowing hard, she had to force herself to go toward him. Before she'd taken more than a few steps into the kitchen, Nick turned. It was little comfort that he didn't look as if he'd had any better a night than she'd had.

His hair was damp from a recent shower or swim, and deep lines were etched at the corners of his mouth. "Good morning," he said in a low, rough voice, his hazel eyes narrowed on her.

She looked away from him to the stove and two covered pans. The coffeepot was perking and two pieces of toast had popped up in the toaster. "What are you doing here? I thought you were going to call Mrs. Douglas?"

"Good morning, Nick, and how did you sleep?" he said.

She darted a sharp glance at him. "What?"

"It's called manners, Sam, and that couch was never meant to be used as a real bed. Lousy sleeping conditions."

"Sorry. Now where is Mrs. Douglas?"

"Is this part of being pregnant?"

"Excuse me?"

"Being rude. I bet your husband loves this kind of reception when you wake up."

She crossed to the sink to get a glass of water.

She couldn't stand there and talk about husbands with Nick.

"Who's Owen?"

"Who?"

"Mrs. Douglas said that she couldn't leave Owen alone and Owen doesn't like visitors."

"Oh, Mrs. Douglas's Owen. I didn't know who you were talking about at first."

"And Owen is...?"

"A Naked African Grey Parrot. He's very sensitive. Pulls out his feathers when he gets stressed and he's almost naked on the chest now."

"A parrot?" He shook his head. "That Mrs. Douglas, she's a strange one, isn't she?"

"She's very nice, Nick, and a good neighbor."

"Cheese on the omelette?" he asked, completely changing the subject.

"Hmm?"

He looked at her over his shoulder. "I'll make this simple. I don't remember if you like cheese on your omelette or not. Do you?"

"Yes, but—"

"Fine. Sit down."

"You can't order me around. And you'd better explain why you just didn't leave."

He faced her with a spatula in his hand. "I'm making breakfast. Omelettes, toast and coffee. Now sit down. It's ready."

She stared at him as he turned back to the stove

and started lifting the food out of the pans. She didn't have it in her to argue, and if truth be told, she was very hungry. She sat at the table where Nick had left two glasses of orange juice. As she sipped some of the cool juice, almost immediately, Nick was putting a plate in front of her with a surprisingly appetizing-looking omelette on it.

"I couldn't figure out how to incorporate peanut butter in the menu, so you'll have to suffer. Do you still take your cream with a little coffee?"

"I'm not drinking coffee for a while. The caffeine, it's not good for…for me right now."

"Okay," he said, then sat opposite her and motioned to her food. "Eat it while it's hot."

"Why are you still here and doing all of this?"

"The truth? I've got a conscience."

She knew her eyes must have widened and he cut her off before she could speak.

"No wisecracks about that being an oxymoron—an attorney with a conscience."

She couldn't bear to banter with him on any level. "Nick, what are you talking about?"

"Eat."

While Nick got up and brought the toast over to the table, she began eating the cheese and mushroom omelette. As she reached for her juice, she looked up to find Nick watching her, his food barely touched.

"I never understood how you could eat so much and never gain weight."

She almost said she was eating for two but kept her mouth shut on that subject. Her appetite was satisfied. "That was good. Thank you. I had no idea that you could cook that well."

"As I said last night, we did a lot of things but never talked much, did we?" he asked as he stood and reached for her empty plate.

That was so true it was painful. She pushed back from the table while Nick took the dishes to the sink. If he started washing them, she knew she'd get hysterical. This was all too much for her to bear at the moment, this domesticated Nick. It was an illusion. A delusion.

"You wash dishes, too?"

"KP from military school," he said over his shoulder. "But now I just scrape. I don't wash. Not unless I'm under extreme duress."

"Just leave them, then you can get going."

"Not before we have a talk," he said, wiping his hands on a towel.

If it was about what almost happened last night, she never even wanted to think about it again, much less talk about it. "Nick, there's nothing to talk about. Maybe later. But for now, it's not important."

"Maybe not in the huge scheme of things, but indulge me, okay?"

"You should have left last night."

"I told you I was staying. I don't lie, and I thought you didn't, either."

"What are you talking about?"

"I told you I was going to make sure you got to the doctor without your having to drive. So, if you want me to leave, just tell me how to reach your husband. When he comes, I leave."

She didn't want this, either, and couldn't even find the words to lie. So she stood and went out to the back porch. The day was beautiful and sunny, the morning air clear and crisp.

"Did you hear what I asked you?"

She turned to see that Nick had followed her and knew she wouldn't lie. There was no point. "Yes, I heard you."

"Well, where is your husband?"

"He isn't," she said flatly.

"What?"

She went down the steps, then onto the lawn, heading toward a small gazebo near the property line.

"Sam?"

"There is no husband."

"You told me that—"

"You assumed that I had a husband," she said as she stopped to find him just a foot or so behind her. "I never said I did."

"Why wouldn't I assume?" Nick asked tightly.

He made himself keep his distance, especially when an anger he thought was past returned with a vengeance.

"Why would you?" she returned softly, the clear morning light exposing soft smudges under her eyes and a certain paleness to her skin. Even so, she looked lovely and delicate.

"Why not? Why would I think you'd be pregnant before we even got a divorce? That you were sleeping with some guy that you weren't married to? You were damned sure that wasn't going to happen when we met."

She stepped into the gazebo and picked up a square canvas bag, an easel and a paint box. Then she turned and brushed past him, striding toward the bluffs.

"What are you doing?"

"I'm going to work on the beach. Thanks for everything," she called without looking back. "I'm fine. You go back to work, too. I'll call and make an appointment in a few months, and we can have a discussion about stuff. See you."

He didn't move for a long moment, then he was hitting a brisk stride to catch up with her. When he was within a few feet, he said, "What in the hell do you think you're doing?"

She didn't stop. "I told you, I'm going to work."

Without another word, he took the easel from

her, then the paint box. "That bag is yours," he said, then started toward the beach. "Which way?"

"I can handle this."

"Which way?" he asked again.

She turned south, and he fell in beside her. They walked in silence, and he could tell she was angry, but he didn't care. He still had something to say. And she'd probably be even angrier when the words were spoken. They went down the beach, past an outcropping of rocks, then into a small cove.

"Here," she said, taking the easel from him. She set it up, propped the canvas bag on it, then held out her hand for the paint box. "I'll take that," she said.

Nick handed it to her, but he didn't leave. He watched while she undid the canvas, laid out the partially finished painting, then opened her paint box on the sand. Without looking at Nick, she reached for the paint palette from the top of the box and would have opened a tube of white paint if Nick hadn't touched her arm.

She immediately moved away from his touch. "What?"

He drew back, narrowed his eyes, then shook his head. "Nothing."

She waited, sure he was going to start something again, but he didn't. Instead, he touched her cheek fleetingly with the tips of his fingers, then silently walked away from her.

Just like that. He left. She turned from the sight of him disappearing around the rock outcropping and found that the painting on the easel was blurring. "Damn hormones," she muttered, swiping at her eyes, then reaching for her palette. "Damn Nick."

NICK WALKED WITHOUT stopping, taking the steps up the bluff two at a time and heading for the house to get his things. He didn't need this. He didn't want this. He stepped through the front door and almost ran into Mrs. Douglas.

"Oh, Mr. Viera, you scared me for a second," she said, pressing one hand over her heart. Then she smiled. "But it's lovely to see you here." She was dressed in jeans, a baggy top and the floppy straw hat from yesterday. She was still wearing running shoes. "I was afraid that you might have left."

"I'll be leaving soon," he said.

"You can't go." She looked almost pained. "No, no, that won't do. You said that Samantha had to go and see the doctor, and you know, she's one of the worst drivers I've ever seen. I mean, I never drove in my life, but dear Norman, my late husband, he drove. A male thing, you know. But Samantha, well, she's quite unsafe driving."

"She's doing better," he said, and went past her into the house to get his laptop and put it in its case. When Sam shut him out on the beach, he'd decided to take the out she'd given him. She'd asked him to leave often enough. He would do what she wanted. He didn't understand anything around here anymore, least of all Sam and himself. "I need to get going. Maybe you can check on Sam a little later. She's on the beach now, painting."

"Alone?"

"She wanted to be alone."

Mrs. Douglas was right behind him. "Dear, no, that's not good. What if she gets dizzy down there? What if she falls on the rocks." She clucked with disapproval. "What if the tide suddenly comes up and—"

"Okay, I get the idea. Why don't you go down and keep her company?"

"Oh, I can't. Owen isn't doing well. He's had a terrible setback. All his tail feathers are gone now." She shook her head. "Poor dear, he just can't deal with life."

The bird wasn't the only one who couldn't deal with his life. "I need to get going. I've got work to—" His cell phone on the table started ringing and he reached out to pick it up. "Yes?"

"Nick, Greg here. How's it going with those depo questions?"

"Why?"

"The London people are open to them. But they need them notarized and in the hands of their attorney by five today. Can you do it?"

He'd tried to work last night, but he knew most of what he did was garbage. "If I could get to London by five, sure, why not?"

"They'll take a fax as long as the hard copy is in their hands in three days. So fax them a notarized copy, then we'll next-day them the hard copy. How about it?"

"Sure, no problem." He could fake what he didn't have. "Five o'clock?"

"Yeah, at the latest, and send it via their London office to Brazelton's attention."

"Okay. Let them know to expect it."

"What's going on?" Greg asked unexpectedly.

Nick was more than aware of Mrs. Douglas standing there, fiddling with the silk flowers on the breakfront, but obviously listening. "A lot of stuff. I'll fill you in later, okay?"

"It's Sam?"

"Very bright man."

"And you can't talk."

"Even brighter. I owe you a bonus."

"Is it good or bad?"

"It's nothing I want," he said. Then saw Mrs. Douglas turn and look at him with a frown. "I need to go. Take care of that and I'll take care of things at my end.''

"You got it," Greg said, then hung up.

Nick flipped the phone shut, then spoke to Mrs. Douglas. "My partner. There's business I have to take care of."

"Oh, legal things? Criminals and such?"

"Sort of. Do you know if there's a notary pubic in town?"

"Of course. Sarah Thompson. In the courthouse. She's been doing the job for years. Used to do it in the post office, but they moved her over to the courthouse. Then she married a judge, if you can believe it, and suddenly she's got a big fancy office." She pursed her lips, then her eyes widened. "Say, your partner, is he perhaps able to handle a land dispute?"

"No, Greg does criminal law, too."

"Oh, well, it can't hurt to ask. If you ever find out about someone who could handle that, you will call me, won't you?"

"If I ever do, I will." He looked at his things, then back at Mrs. Douglas. "Why did you come by?"

"Oh, the soup. It's in the kitchen. You make sure that Samantha gets a big bowl of it, won't you?"

Hadn't she heard him say he was leaving? Or hadn't she believed him? "I'm leaving, and—"

"Mr. Viera, I can tell that you're a kind man. You wouldn't still be here if you didn't care about Samantha. Now, I think you're going to do the right thing and make sure she gets that soup, also make sure she gets to the doctor." She smiled. "The courthouse is right down the street from the doctor's office. Two birds with one stone, you know what I mean?"

He knew exactly. "Okay, you win. I'll make sure she gets to the doctor, then I'll be leaving. I might not see you again, so you take care and thanks for the soup."

"Oh, we'll meet again," she said. "Now, I have to go home and tend to Owen. You take care of yours and I'll take care of mine." She winked at him, then turned and left.

Nick wondered why he felt as if he'd been flim-flammed by an elderly lady in a floppy hat. Because he had been? He was doing what she wanted him to do so she could go home and take care of a parrot without tail feathers. He switched on his laptop, opened his file on the questions, then started to work on the revisions.

But no more than five minutes had gone by before he closed the computer and went out the front door. Mrs. Douglas had talked about Sam's getting dizzy, falling on the rocks. He couldn't get those thoughts out of his mind. God, he was beginning to feel like Sam's protector. He hadn't even felt that way when they were married.

SAM WAS LOST IN HER WORK, painting a tiny child frolicking in the surf, a golden-haired child whose face was filled with delight. She glanced up to gaze at the shoreline and her brush stilled. A swimmer just beyond the breakwater was heading toward shore. Nick. She recognized him immediately and watched him swimming into shallow water.

As he stood in calf-deep water, Sam had one clear thought—that she was thankful he wasn't running true to form. He wasn't naked. He had on shorts of some sort. No, they were white boxers, wet and hiding very little. She saw him shake his head, then rake his fingers through his hair as he stepped out of the water onto the sand.

"How's it going?" he called as he walked toward her.

She stared at him, finally realizing that what she should be thinking about was the fact that he was still here. And she shouldn't be thinking about him wearing that piece of clinging cotton and how it was almost more indecent than if he'd been naked. "What are you still doing here?" she asked, feeling proud that she'd managed to get the question out and make sense.

"Taking a swim. I didn't realize how much I miss the ocean when I'm not in Malibu." He ran a hand roughly over his face as he stopped behind the easel and looked at her over the top. "It's been too long and the ocean is so enticing."

"You were swimming last night," she said before she could stop herself, then wished she could take back the words when a slow, seductive smile touched his lips.

"You were peeking?" he asked in a low, suggestive voice.

"I was not. I was…" She abruptly reached down for the cleaning rag to start on her brushes. "I was just looking at the ocean. I didn't know you'd decided to take a swim. So it hasn't been that long," she said, scrubbing at a brush before putting it in the bottle with thinner.

"Okay, so I was swimming last night. I thought another swim would be a good idea."

She turned to him, but he'd moved and was at the side of the easel, studying her painting. "You should have packed swimming trunks," she said.

Why did she say that? Especially when a wicked glint came into his eyes along with a lifting of his lips. "I was considering swimming in my birthday suit, but realized you've got a neighbor who, by the way, brought you some soup for lunch."

"Mrs. Douglas?"

"Yes. She had to get home to Owen. It seems he plucked his tail clean last night, poor thing."

She could almost believe that they were two old

friends who'd met and talked and were at ease with each other. But that was so far from the truth it was almost laughable. "I thought you had gone—especially after last night."

He waved that aside. "You always think I'm gone, but I'm not," he said. "Last night—well—I'm sorry."

Sorry? She swallowed hard, thankful "sorry" could cover what almost happened. "You always *say* you're leaving, but you *don't*."

"A bad habit, I guess," he said, then looked back at her painting and let out a low whistle. "This is fantastic. It's…it's magical. No wonder you're doing so well." He glanced at her again, his eyes narrowed against the brightness of the early-afternoon sun. "I'm impressed, Sam, very impressed."

She didn't want his approval. "It's not finished. I hoped to finish it today, but…" She started to reach for the canvas to pack up and return to the house.

"Don't," Nick said.

She frowned at him as she drew back her hand. "Don't what?"

"Don't stop. From the looks of it, you're on a roll."

"You're leaving?"

He nodded, but any relief she experienced was

short-lived. "In a while. I actually came down here to get some information from you."

She could feel that sense of being out of control creeping back into her, and it was all because of this man. "What now?"

Unexpectedly, he touched her chin with the tip of his finger. He was so close she could actually smell the ocean on his skin. And the boxers were drying, clinging to him in an even more outrageous way. She couldn't take this situation much longer, not his closeness or the contact from his fingers that felt suspiciously like fire on her skin.

"I need a notary public," he said.

"Sorry, I paint," she replied, shifting her head away from his touch. "I don't notarize anything. Can't *you* notarize things?"

He chuckled softly as he lowered his hand. "I didn't think you did. And I can't notarize anything with my own signature on it, even if I were a notary public. But Mrs. Douglas mentioned that some woman named Sarah something-or-other in town can do it."

She hated the way a smile was lingering around his lips. She admitted one thing about Nicholas Viera, one very important thing—he could be so damned endearing. The way he'd been when she first met him. Dangerous ground, very dangerous ground, with a man who likened marriage to the prisons he'd worked to get his clients out of all his professional life.

"It seems you know what you need to know, so what information do you need from me?" she asked.

"How far is the courthouse from the doctor's office? Mrs. Douglas said it's a short distance, but then again, the lady has a bird that eats its own feathers."

"It's right down the street. Why do you need one?"

"I have to get some documents notarized by five today. The way I figure it, I can drive you into town, drop you at the doctor's, get the papers notarized, and everyone's happy."

"God, you're stubborn," she muttered.

"No, just looking at things logically. Your driving gives me fits, and—"

"Okay, whoa, stop right there. I drive just fine," she said. "I've done all my own driving since I was sixteen, and despite my track record with your cars and my one court appearance, I've done okay. I got you back to the house in Malibu without incident." She paused and had to swallow hard when she thought of the "incident" that happened after they were in the house together. "Even if you don't remember it, I took you home and I drove that car of yours. Not a scratch on it, either."

That only brought back the smile. "Okay, okay,

you made your point," he said, and the smile faded. "But what if you get dizzy while you're driving? That's not something you want to take a chance on, is it?"

Logic again. Painting her into a corner with his words. He was a lawyer even in personal arguments. She sighed, knowing that resisting like this was going nowhere. She didn't want him standing there, looking like some sea god telling her what she should or shouldn't do. "Oh, all right, you can drive me. I'll work some more and be up to the house in a while. Then we can go. You can get your stuff done, and I can see the doctor, and you should be leaving Jensen Pass behind around six o'clock." She reached for another brush. "How's that?"

"Perfect," he murmured, looking at her long and hard. "How long do you think you'll be here?"

It had to be around two, so she said, "Another hour."

"Perfect," he said again.

She expected him to do one of two things—go back to the water and dive in to swim back or head off across the sand to the north. But once again, he didn't do what she expected. He dropped down on the sand beside her and stretched out full length on the beach.

## Chapter Eleven

"Nick, what are you doing?" Sam asked.

He clasped his hands behind his neck and closed his eyes. "You've had too much sun if you don't know what this is. God knows we did it enough in Malibu. It's called sunbathing. Now does it ring a bell?"

She stared at him, words choking in her throat, but nothing coming out. Not when her eyes insisted on slipping along his body, down his chest to his abdomen, then to the pair of cotton boxers he was wearing. She turned quickly, brushed at her eyes and reached for her palette again. "Whatever," she muttered, then dabbed at the paint and furiously began filling in the ocean background with long, serious strokes.

"I knew you'd remember," he murmured.

She worked without talking, never looking over at Nick. It was bad enough he wasn't moving, that he just stayed there stretched out in the sun. But when she finally realized that there was no way she could finish the painting that day, she'd barely dropped her brush in the thinner before Nick was up.

While she slipped her canvas into its carrier, Nick folded up the easel and reached for the canvas bag. "The paint box is all yours."

"Thanks," she muttered, grabbing her paints and finally looking at Nick. Mistake. Again. His skin was darker now, flushed from that short time in the heat and sun, and his eyes were a stunning green-brown. She'd forgotten how easily he tanned. And how hard it was for her to tan. She could feel a bit of sunburn on her arms already.

Without a word, she started back, going along the sand. The trek they'd taken on the way to the cove was repeated in reverse, but this time Nick wasn't dressed in his jeans and shirt. Not even close. She kept her eyes on the ground ahead of her and concentrated on where she was going.

"So, we never finished our talk," he said.

That made her falter, but she steadied herself and kept going. "Sorry, we aren't talking."

"Oh, what are we doing?"

"Walking."

"Then why can't we talk?"

"Okay. It's a nice day, clear, not too warm, and the light was perfect and—"

"That's not what I want to talk about."

She walked faster and kept quiet, praying he'd just let it go so this could be over soon. But her prayers didn't stop Nick.

"Sam, would you slow down and listen to me?"

She ignored him as best she could, thankful to see her cottage not far in the distance. But she didn't get much closer to it. Nick reached out and stopped her by grabbing her upper arm.

"I want to talk, Sam."

She closed her eyes tightly. "Too bad. We don't always get what we want, do we?" That was the painful truth she'd learned early in life. Right around the time she'd had to leave her first foster home. And her most recent lesson had been when she realized she would never have Nick. "That's life."

"Bull," he muttered, letting her go when she twisted her arm.

Sam noticed the intensity in his expression. "Nick, there's nothing left to say. You should have left before."

"Damn right, I should have, but I couldn't." He looked angry then, furious, in fact.

"Of course you can. I told you to go. But you won't listen to me, not about anything."

"Oh, I've listened to you before. I've listened to you tell me that you wanted the whole ball of wax—marriage, a home, a family. I listened."

"It must have sounded like a foreign language

to you,'' she said, not wanting to fight about this again but unable to just let it go.

He took a deep breath, then asked abruptly, ''Why did you do it?''

Frustration choked her. ''I left you because—''

He held up his hand. ''That's not it. Just tell me why you changed. Why you went against everything you kept telling me you valued.'' His hand closed into a fist as he lowered it. ''How could you get pregnant like that? And where in the hell is the guy now? Why isn't he with you?''

Sam narrowed her eyes, surprising herself with what she said next. ''What if someone walked up to you and said, 'Guess what, Nick, you're going to be a father'? What would you do?''

He shook his head. ''That's ridiculous.''

''Indulge me with this hypothetical question. You understand hypothetical questions. What would you do?'' she asked, holding her breath waiting for his answer.

He shrugged. ''I don't know.''

''You don't want kids, do you?''

''No, but if there was a mistake, it could be corrected.''

She grimaced at his choice of words but knew that's just what he'd eventually do. He'd try to correct the mistake. ''That's it?''

''What did the father say about that?'' he asked, motioning to her stomach.

"I didn't tell him yet."

"What are you waiting for—the kid to graduate from college?"

"Maybe, or maybe just until it's here and safe and healthy. I don't know." She really didn't know when she'd tell him. "When it feels right, I'll tell him."

"Why are you keeping it?"

"Because I want this baby. My getting pregnant was an accident. I made love with him that one time, and it was crazy, but it happened." She could feel tears burning at the back of her eyes and fought them like mad as she touched her stomach. "I never imagined things would turn out like this." She bit her lip hard. "Then when they did, I never thought of not going through with it."

"Alone?"

She hated Nick for asking her all these questions, his words exposing the isolation she'd always felt. "I've been alone most of my life, so this isn't much different."

"It's as different as night from day," he muttered.

"Nick, I don't want to talk about any of this with you."

"I guess you think since I let you go, I gave up my right to worry about you?"

"You *let* me go? I left." She couldn't keep the

bitterness out of her tone. "You didn't do anything. You never even came after me."

His expression tightened, but he didn't argue. "No matter what I did or didn't do then, you can't go through all of this alone."

"Of course I can. I don't have a choice, do I?"

"There are always choices."

"What choices? Begging the father to be part of the baby's life, to do what he not only doesn't want to do, but also couldn't do to save his life? I have to do this on my own and I'm used to it. I don't need your help or anyone else's help."

Sam turned away from Nick and headed up the bluff. She could hear the sound of the ocean in the distance, the slight sighing of the breeze building as her own breathing began to grow more rapid.

"One choice would have been for you to stay with me," Nick said, his voice close behind her.

That was so beyond reality that it was almost funny. Almost. The pain his words caused ripped at her and she turned to face him. "Stay with you? God, you hated our marriage. You hated being 'caught.' You hated the impulse that made you agree to marry me. How could I have stayed with you when you didn't want me?"

"I've never stopped wanting you," he said in a low, rough voice.

"I'm not talking about lust, about going to bed together. I'm talking about building a life together.

That wasn't even an option. You made that very clear.''

He raked his fingers through his hair. "Damn it, Sam, life isn't all neat and orderly. Things happen, and you have to deal with them."

"No kidding," she muttered, the bitterness growing into a flare of anger. "In case you didn't notice, that's what I'm doing."

"I know, I know." He ran one hand around the back of his neck and grimaced ruefully. "I just wish we could go back before all this craziness happened."

She almost laughed at that, but knew if she did it wouldn't be laughter that consumed her; it would be hysteria. "It doesn't work that way, Nick. Life doesn't rewind just for you."

"No, but we can be friends, can't we? We can still see each other. I've missed you, you know. Just because we couldn't make our marriage work, does that mean we can't—"

"We can't sleep together? What? You go your way, I go mine, but every once in a while, we have sex? We have nothing in common. Nothing in our lives mesh, but every so often we get together? What do you call that?"

"I call it not losing you completely."

That did bring a laugh, a bitter sound that made her almost cringe. "Too late. Way too late," she said. "Sorry, you lose. This isn't something you can talk your way into getting. You're losing your touch, Nick.''

He threw up his hand in obvious exasperation. ''God, you can't even talk reasonably, can you?''

''Me? How dare you even suggest something like you just suggested?''

''*I* didn't suggest *anything*. You twisted it around.''

She closed her eyes, trying to control the rage churning inside her, rage that bred a pain she could barely deal with at that moment. ''I can't do this. I *won't* do this.''

''Who is he?''

Her eyes flew open. ''Won't you ever stop?''

''Who is he?''

''It doesn't matter.''

''It mattered enough for you to sleep with him, so I guess he matters, or at least mattered once. Hell, I had to marry you,'' he said tightly.

He was destroying everything for her. Shattering all the peace she'd so recently found. Irrational fury ripped through her, and before she knew what she was going to do, her hand swung out at him. There was a stinging moment of shock, and the slap seemed to echo all around them.

She drew her hand back, balling her fingers into her smarting palm, and stared at Nick in horror. ''You...you're ruining everything, and I...I want you to get out of here now.''

He never touched his face even though she could see the imprint of her open hand beginning to flare on his cheek. He just stood very still before he said in a low voice, "I've tried."

"Try harder," she snapped, and turned away from him, her throat clenching, her eyes burning. She wanted to be as far from him as she could be before she cried. She hadn't cried for years, but she hadn't been able to stop crying for the past twenty-four hours.

Once she got to the cottage and went inside, Sam ignored the couch where Nick had slept, where his things were still lying on the small end table, and went straight upstairs. She made it to the bathroom and closed the door behind her. Without glancing at the mirror, she stripped off her clothes, turned on the shower and stepped under the fine spray.

Holding her still-tingling hand under the water she tried to stop her tears. She hadn't meant to hit Nick and she didn't want to cry again. But she *was* crying and she *had* struck Nick.

"Damn it, damn it, damn it," she muttered as she lifted her face to the stream of water until her tears were lost in the flow.

WHEN NICK STEPPED INTO the cottage, he heard movement upstairs, then water start to run. If he'd been in court instead of on the beach with Sam, he would have lost his case because he'd let himself get crazy. He'd let his ego take over and he'd let his gut do the thinking instead of his head.

He crossed to his things beside the couch, grabbed fresh clothes out of his overnight case, then headed for the downstairs bathroom. Bitterness engulfed him, and his regret was overwhelming. He stepped into the tiny bathroom and looked in the mirror over the sink. He could still make out the imprint of Sam's hand on his cheek.

Damn it, he'd deserved that slap. She was right. He was way out of line. He was so far over the top in his reactions to everything about Sam that it was scary. As he touched his cheek, the memory of the pain in Sam's eyes just before she struck out burned into him. He hadn't wanted it to end this way.

What a mess he'd made. Sam thought he wanted to take her to bed, then walk away. She thought that was *all* he wanted from her.

His stomach knotted. A thought suddenly occurred to him. He *had* wanted more from Sam from the first time he met her; he just hadn't realized it until this moment. But, even so, he wasn't certain what he wanted. Making love to Sam was something he still craved, but that desire was now blurred by a need to protect her, to take care of her, to sit and look at her as she worked. To be close and inhale the delicate scent that seemed to surround her and entice him whenever she was near.

He was stark raving mad. And he knew it. This cottage and Sam had cast a spell over him. Even the idea of his ex-wife's having another man's child hadn't killed the growing need Nick had for her. No matter how he tried to rationalize his feelings, he couldn't rationalize away the fact that he didn't want to let her go completely; he never did.

SAM STAYED IN HER ROOM until half an hour before her doctor's appointment. She took her time changing into a white smock-front dress with spaghetti straps and a softly pleated, calf-length skirt. The locket was at her throat, and she touched it lovingly, happy to have it with her again.

She slipped her shoes on, feeling a touch of nausea. She hadn't felt sick for a while, since the weeks following her return from Los Angeles. Then, she'd thought she had the flu, and that belief had gone on for two weeks, the days of sickness interspersed with days of feeling terrific.

A flu that persisted, she'd thought, until she realized it wasn't normal. Other things caught her attention, as well, and even before she'd gone to the doctor's, she'd suspected what was "wrong" with her. She'd had unprotected sex with Nick only one time and it had only taken that one time for her to conceive Nick's child.

Taking a deep breath to calm herself, she stood and smoothed her dress over her stomach. The baby stirred and the sensation was as awesome as it had been the first time. But now Nick was gone. She reached for her purse, got out her car keys, then headed downstairs.

Expecting quiet and emptiness, she stepped into the parlor and instead found Nick sitting on the couch. He'd changed into a gray shirt and dark slacks. His hair was slicked back damply from his face. He was working on his laptop, but looked up at her as she came into the room.

The man's presence robbed her of the most elementary ability to speak. She watched him close the computer and put it in a black carrying case before he finally spoke. "I thought you were going to be late. I was beginning to think I needed to go up and get you."

She finally found her voice and came farther into the room, but she kept a good space between herself and the man watching her to act as a buffer zone. She wasn't surprised to see him there—he couldn't surprise her anymore. "I feel as if I'm always asking you why you're here."

"It's because you are," he said without a smile as he stood. "And I've got a problem."

She felt a niggling sense of relief that he hadn't left with the slap and harsh words hanging between them. "What problem?"

"I'm getting in the habit of apologizing to you every time I turn around, and it's going to ruin my reputation if it gets out."

"Apologizing for what?"

He shrugged, his shoulders tugging at the fine fabric of his shirt. "I'm sorry for what I said down on the beach. I had no right."

His apology took her off balance. "I hit you. I should be the one apologizing."

"No, I'm lucky you didn't strangle me."

"I'm just so damned…" She bit her lip. "My emotions are way off-kilter lately."

"You won't get an argument from me about that," he said, a suggestion of a smile on his lips as he rubbed his jaw. "To make it up to you, I'm driving you into town, getting my business done, getting you back here, then I'll give you your wish. I'll leave. I'll get the hell of out of town by sunset."

"Do you really mean it this time?"

"Yes. I think we both know it's time."

He'd said what she thought she'd wanted to hear since he appeared out of the blue yesterday. But instead of happiness over knowing he was leaving soon, she felt tears behind her eyes. Pregnancy was making her crazy and she found herself nervously fingering her locket. "Yes, it's time," she whispered. And it was time, for she wouldn't let herself think about what could happen if he didn't keep his promise to leave.

"Let's get this over with," Nick said as he opened the door for her.

The words sounded so final, and she could do little more than nod as she moved past him to the porch. Nick followed her, carrying his computer and overnight case. She stopped to close the door, then crossed to his rental car.

"Nice wheels," she remarked as she got in.

"Nothing like a convertible," Nick said as he slid behind the wheel.

She looked away, anywhere but at Nick. This wasn't what she wanted or where she wanted to be. But she had to admit that driving herself would have been a scary proposition.

"How are you feeling?" Nick asked as he turned onto the main road. "Any more dizziness?"

"No. I think it was just from not eating," she said, not adding that the shock of his being there was probably an even more direct cause of all her turmoil.

They drove down the road, the air rushing past, the sky so blue that she knew she couldn't have duplicated the color with paints.

"It's a beautiful afternoon," she said.

She felt Nick turn to her, but she kept her face lifted to the sun and let the air play with her hair. "Yes, beautiful," he said.

"And not too warm, either," she said.

"Are you going to give the farm report now?" he asked.

She looked at him. "I'm making conversation," she said.

"If you don't want to talk about anything important, I can live with that." He touched his face. "I don't need to have you slug me again."

"I really am sorry about that. I guess I just…well, lost control."

"No problem," he murmured, then grew silent as they approached the town.

Sam was the one to break the silence as they neared the center of Jensen Pass. She pointed to the courthouse, an old rambling building with white columns and an impressive staircase that led to a massive entry. "That's the courthouse. You'll find Sarah in there."

"Okay. Now where's the doctor's office?"

"He's not far from the courthouse." Nick drove down the street, and Sam pointed to the doctor's office house in a huge old bungalow. "There."

He pulled into a gravel parking area in front of the house, got out and came around the car. Sam hurried to get out, then started for the entry with Nick beside her. He pushed the door open for her, then she stepped into the reception area that had once been the original home's parlor.

Maria, Dr. Barnet's nurse, crossed to Sam immediately. "We'll take good care of Samantha," she said to Nick.

"I have some business to look after. When do you think she'll be done?" he asked.

"Give us half an hour. The doctor's free, so he can see her right away."

"Okay, I'll be back then." Sam nodded without turning and heard the door shut behind Nick. Then Maria accompanied her back to one of the examining rooms. Half an hour later, she was leaving the examining room with Dr. Barnet. His words, just moments earlier, had startled her tremendously.

"You're showing quite a bit for only being four months along and you're measuring larger than most," he'd told her. "Are there any cases of multiple births in your family or the father's family?"

As she and the doctor stepped into the waiting room, she saw Nick, standing there with his back against the wall, just watching her. He glanced at the doctor and came forward, his hand held out. "I'm Nick Viera, the one who called you yesterday. How's Sam?"

The men shook hands as the doctor spoke. "Nothing to worry about, but she has to be careful to eat on a regular basis. And she needs to get some information for me, but other than that, things look great."

Nick looked at Sam. "Ready to go?"

"Yes," she said as she walked to the door and stepped outside.

"What do you need to find out?" he asked as they neared the car.

"If there are twins in the family," she said, hugging herself.

Nick opened the car door for her and she slipped inside. When he got in behind the wheel, she glanced over at him to find him staring at her. "Twins?" He grimaced. "Two at once?"

"That's what twins usually are, Nick. And don't look so pained."

"I'm not pained." He hesitated. "Okay, okay, maybe a little." Without warning, he reached out and lightly patted her stomach, an achingly intimate action that almost brought tears to her eyes. "Two Sams. That's not all bad."

She turned away from him, shocked that all she wanted to do right then was to keep his hand nestled on her stomach. She was thankful he'd be leaving soon.

## Chapter Twelve

Nick had no idea why he'd touched Sam so lovingly or why he didn't apologize for it. Instead, he gripped the steering wheel and kept driving.

"If it is twins, at least it wouldn't be an only child like you were," Sam was saying.

"My parents believed in doing it once and doing it right," he said, trying to break the tension with a joke, but it didn't work for either of them.

"No twins in your family, I take it?"

"No. They wouldn't have dared to appear," he said.

The whole situation he'd fallen into yesterday with Sam was still eating at him, and his confusion was only intensified as he stole a look at her again when he stopped at a red light. She looked so very delicate, almost ethereal. Her hair was slightly mussed, and a frown tugged at her finely drawn brows as she looked straight ahead.

A cold, hard fact suddenly hit him in his gut and

wouldn't let go. She was lost to him completely despite what had almost happened the night before. She'd moved on. She'd found someone else even if it had only been for a brief time. She was having a child.

He'd never understood the concept of love. He didn't think he'd ever told any woman in his life that he loved her, or ever heard the words said to him. But what he felt for Sam, or what he used to feel for her, probably came as close to love as anything in his life ever had. Need. Want. Desire. He understood all those feelings, feelings that had been very real in his relationship with Sam. And when he looked at her, he experienced those emotions again. One touch, and they were all there, burning brightly and intensely. But love?

He glanced across the road to the courthouse and realized how damned distracted Sam had made him. He'd walked out of Sarah Thompson's office without his computer. They'd let him print out his documents by hooking his computer up to their printer, and he'd left it sitting there. "Damn it," he muttered, and turned into a parking spot near the front of the courthouse.

"What's wrong?"

He turned to Sam. "I forgot my computer. Wait here. I won't be very long."

She undid her seat belt and reached for the door handle. "I won't be very long, either."

"You don't need..."

She looked at him, her eyes shadowed by her lashes. "I need a rest room."

"But you were just at the doctor's and—"

"I still have to use the bathroom again. Eating peanut butter out of the jar isn't the only peculiar side effect of being pregnant. I won't make it back home and there's a rest room in the courthouse. I'll meet you back here in a few minutes."

Inside the building, she motioned to her left. "The rest rooms are down there. See you in a minute." And she headed down the hallway, her sandals tapping softly on the highly polished hardwood floors.

He watched her go past closed doors, and when she turned to her right and disappeared, he realized that he was falling into a dangerous situation. It wasn't the physical thing. Even if he never touched her again, he could deal with that by taking a cold shower and never sleeping. But he was starting to experience a horrible case of overprotectiveness. In fact, it was his first case.

He turned and went down the hall in the opposite direction. He'd actually thought of going with her to the ladies' room, making sure she found the right door and didn't get dizzy again. It was insane. Sam could take care of herself and certainly didn't need him. That brought a humorless chuckle from him as he reached the door of the notary public.

Sam had done a good job of getting pregnant all on her own.

He stepped into the office, and saw Sarah sitting at her huge mahogany desk. She was a heavyset woman, given to wearing all black. "I was just getting ready to call out the marines," she said with a big smile as she reached under the desk and lifted out his laptop. "Not that I wouldn't like a machine like this, but they frown on keeping lost items around here."

"Sorry I forgot it," he said.

She looked up at him as he took the computer. "You attorneys are all the same, always preoccupied with cases. If it wasn't fastened to your shoulders, you'd forget your heads. My husband's like that, you know," she said, her purple lipstick stretching with a smile. "He's just thinking about so much, so distracted, that he'd forget to wear his pants if I didn't remind him to put them on before he left the house in the morning."

He laughed politely, then said, "Thanks, I appreciate it." Before she could start up again, he went in search of Sam.

He stepped out into the hallway and heard noises coming from the other wing. Suddenly, there was a scream and the sound of running feet pounding on the hardwood floor. He hurried toward the commotion, turned the corner and barely avoided a group of men and women running in the opposite direction.

"Don't go down there," one of the men in shirt-sleeves yelled.

Then a middle-aged woman came running toward him, holding her purse to her middle and looking scared out of her wits. "What's going on?" Nick asked, grabbing her by her arm to stop her for a second.

She pulled free, crying, "Some crazy guy's holding a woman hostage in there. He's got the policeman's gun and he'd threatening to kill everyone!"

A fear that he'd never experienced in his life flooded through Nick. Something told him Sam was in danger. Maybe she'd been trapped by the situation or she was hiding somewhere, terrified.

Then two uniformed policemen rushed up behind him, almost knocking him into the wall. "Get out of here," one of them shouted at him, but he didn't move. He watched them racing down the length of the hallway, then turn right. He barely hesitated before following them. He rounded the corner and saw a blur of uniforms by a door marked Criminal Court 2.

He went closer and stopped dead as he looked past a ring of cops with their guns drawn. Sam. A man had her—a man in a jailhouse-orange jump-suit, a man who couldn't have been more than twenty, with wild eyes, long black hair and a gun pressed just below Sam's ear.

The guy had pinned her in front of him, his forearm pressed over her throat so tightly that her whole body arched backward. She was hyperventilating, gripping his arm with one hand, her other hand clutching her middle.

A bomb going off couldn't have rocked Nick's world any more than the sight of Sam. He couldn't even find a word to explain how he felt right then as a nauseating fear grew within him. Not thinking of what he was doing, he tried to get to her, but as he took a step forward, one of the cops stopped him.

"Get out of here," the officer ordered, and moved his body to block him.

Nick backed up but didn't leave. Through the press of policemen he could see Sam flinch when the guy screamed, "You all get back or I'll blow her brains out. I ain't got nothin' to lose!"

The ring of cops retreated a few feet. It looked like a standoff. Nick had never been at a loss for anything in his life, but at that moment, his mind refused to focus. All he could see was Sam, the sheer terror in her eyes, the tears that flowed silently down her cheeks and the way she protectively held her stomach.

Nick looked at the cop closest to him, who was holding a court file. He read the name typed on the tab along with an arrest number. Louis Franco. Setting his computer on the floor, he reached into his pocket for his wallet. He took out a business card and pushed it in front of the cop with the clipboard. "Franco's one of mine," he lied.

As the cop took the card, Nick broke through the circle of officers and approached Franco before anyone around him knew what he was doing.

He sensed the cops moving toward him, but he stopped them by holding up his hands, palms open to Franco. "Take it easy, Louis. I'm not armed and I'm here to help you."

The young man fell back a foot, dragging Sam with him until he was against the wall. "What in the…?"

Nick lowered his hands slightly, pressing the open palms toward the hostage taker. "Just calm down. You don't want to hurt anyone. Believe me, you don't want that on your record."

Nick slowly inched forward, stopping about six feet away. He made very sure that he didn't look at Sam. He wasn't sure what he'd do if he looked into her eyes. At that moment, he needed all his wits about him.

"Louis, hold on, hold on," he said when he saw the hand holding the gun start to tense. "Calm down. Take a breath. Things are going to get a hell of a lot worse if you don't listen to me."

"Why should I? I ain't gonna get out of here

anyway. They're pinning a third strike on me, and I'm gone. It's over. Twenty-five to life. Gone.''

Nick tried to focus on the guy, knowing that he had to gain his confidence if he was going to help Sam. ''Who told you that?''

''My freebie, the public pretender.''

''A public defender?''

''Yeah, call 'em what you want. They ain't doing me no good. He's telling me I gotta plea out to felony assault. It was a fight, self-defense, and he says I gotta take the rap for it. I get my third strike and the other guy gets off. Well, that ain't gonna happen, not in this life. I ain't goin' down for no one. He pulled a knife on me, and I got it and cut him. Self-defense, man, self-defense!''

''If what you're saying is the truth, you shouldn't plea out on it. No way,'' Nick said, getting even closer. ''I wouldn't let you.''

Franco blinked, and Nick knew he had crossed that invisible line. The guy was listening to him and believing him. Or at least, he wanted to believe him. ''What?''

''You got bad advice, believe me. All you need is a good attorney and a plea to a misdemeanor, you'd do a year, get out and it's done.''

The gun lowered a fraction of an inch, and Nick had to force himself not to react. It was all he could do not to reach out and grab for Sam when he heard her utter a soft sob. It made his heart lurch, but he needed to stay cool. He had to keep in control.

"What do you know?" Franco asked, but he didn't sound as sure. "You're just saying things to—"

Nick cut him off. "I know exactly what I'm saying. I'm an attorney, specializing in criminal law. I'm damned good at it. I can tell you, if you stop this now, I promise you'll have the best attorney I can get for you. I'll work this out and it won't have to go any further."

"How…how do I know you ain't lying to me?" the young man asked, his voice touched by desperation. He wanted an out and all Nick had to do was say the right words.

Sam gasped again, and Nick instinctively looked at her. He knew then that he'd do or say anything to put an end to this horror. He had to force himself to look back at Franco. "You're going to have to trust me on this, Louis. I know an attorney in San Francisco who I'll make sure will take your case. Martin Swicker. He's good."

Then he found himself saying something he never would have if the hostage had been anyone but Sam. "If you let her go and do it now, you've got my word that Swicker will be here and he'll take care of you. It's your choice."

"What's all this to you?" Franco asked.

Nick looked at Sam and his words were stark

and simple. "She's my wife, and she's pregnant. And if you do anything to hurt her or the child, you're dead. If you let her go, you'll get the best help money can buy. What's it going to be, Louis?"

Nick held his breath while the desperate young man looked frantically around, then back at him. Had he overplayed his hand? Had he let his emotions ruin everything?

"Get Swicker," Franco said finally, slowly lowering the gun and letting it clatter to the floor. A second later, the world exploded with action.

Nick reached for Sam, grabbing her to him. A multitude of cops jumped on top of Franco, pinning him to the floor, handcuffing then pulling him back to his feet. Nick held tightly to Sam, burying her face in his chest and letting her cry. And over her head, he met the hostage taker's eyes.

"You'll keep your word?" Franco asked.

Nick nodded. "Count on it."

The cops twisted the guy away, but not before he shouted, "Louis Franco, don't forget my name's Louis Franco!"

Nick watched them take Franco away, then exhaled in a rush. He was holding on to Sam for dear life and her whole body was shaking. He was shaking too, and had to close his eyes for a long moment to regain some kind of composure.

Cops surrounded them, and one placed his arm

on Nick's shoulder. "You took a hell of a chance, mister," the cop said. "That punk's all freaked out. Never even saw him make a break for it before he had my partner's gun and was out the door. Then he grabbed the lady as she came out of the rest room, and all hell broke loose."

Nick felt Sam take a convulsive breath and held her even tighter. "It's over, it's over," he murmured to her.

"Yeah, he's not going anywhere soon," the cop said. Then he patted Nick on the shoulder. "Nice job. He bought your story hook, line and sinker."

Nick didn't need or want the man's praise. He only cared that Sam was there in one piece, safe and sound in his arms. In that moment, he finally understood something. Love. A part of love had to be that feeling of fear at the thought of losing someone. That aching agony when he envisioned a world without that person in it. He'd sure as hell felt that and more in the past few minutes, and he felt them all because of Sam. It might not be love, but he suspected it was as close as he'd ever get to such an emotion in his life. And it was too late.

"Swicker will be in touch about him," Nick said.

"Hey, you really meant that?" the cops asked.

"Put Swicker down as his attorney," Nick said, then felt Sam's trembling. "We're leaving. I'm taking her to the doctor's, then home."

"She's really your wife?" the man asked.

"She was," he said, then had a glimmer of what he'd lost when he let her walk out of his life.

"Well, you'll need to talk to the chief, so he can sort this out," the officer said.

"Not now. I gave my card to one of your men. Tell your chief he can contact me in a day or two."

Then he was moving, helping Sam toward the exit and away from the confusion. She leaned against him as they went out into the fresh air, and he never let go of her until they got through the crowd that had gathered and were at the car. Then he helped her into the passenger side, more than aware of the way she all but collapsed in the seat. He hurried around to get behind the wheel and reached for his cell phone.

Holding it out to Sam, he said, "Call the doctor and tell him we'll be there in a minute."

She took the phone but didn't dial the number. "Please, just take me home."

Nick pulled out into traffic, shaking his head. "No way. I told you I don't know a thing about pregnancy, never thought I'd have to, but I know that something like what just happened can be trouble." He tapped the phone in her hand. "Either call him or we'll just burst in. It's your choice."

She pushed in a number, pressed the phone to her ear and told the nurse what had happened.

"The doctor will be waiting for me," she assured Nick when she hung up.

She sank back with a shuddering sigh, and he reached out and grabbed her hand without a second thought. The unsteadiness of her hand unnerved him and he never let go until they were in front of the doctor's again.

Maria was waiting for them at the entrance. She slipped an arm around Sam and started to take her back toward the examination rooms. "The doctor's waiting for you." She looked over her shoulder at Nick. "You can come if you want."

Nick stood by the door and shook his head. He was climbing too far into Sam's life again to feel comfortable, too damn far. "Just take care of her."

Maria nodded and disappeared with Sam. Nick heard the doctor's voice. "Samantha, thank God it's over and—"

His voice was cut off by a door shutting, then Maria returned out front. "Wow, that's just way too much excitement for me," she said as she dropped down behind her desk. She rested both elbows on the desktop and leaned toward Nick. "You seem very concerned about Sam. May I ask what your relationship is?"

"We're divorced," he said, the words blunt and honest, but they felt wrong when he said them.

"Oh, one of those friendly divorces?"

"We're still friends," he said, hoping that was

true and that it would always be true. But he had a gnawing feeling that once he drove away from Jensen Pass, he'd never be back, that she'd never let him back into her life. He hated that thought.

"Good to hear that. I remember thinking how sad it was she was all alone, no husband or anything." Maria's voice dropped lower again. "Oh, not that I'm judging anyone, mind you." Her words echoed Mrs. Douglas's. "Things happen, but she's so beautiful and so talented. I mean, I don't have to tell you, after all you were married to her...but then again, you got divorced."

Yes, he'd married her. The fact that she was beautiful and talented certainly figured into it, along with a lot of other things. Stubborn. She'd wanted him but told him in no uncertain terms that she wasn't about to have some affair. "I'm old-fashioned," she'd said with that endearing blush of hers. "I couldn't be with someone I didn't feel committed to." He'd looked at her, touched her, kissed her, and knew that she could have anything she wanted from him.

"Oh, here they are," Maria said.

"I told you we didn't need to come," Sam said as she drew near.

He looked past her at the doctor. "The baby's okay?"

"It's fine. Samantha's just shaken. We need to be careful for a few days. The only thing I'm not happy with is Samantha's being out at the house alone. I've tried to talk her into hiring a nurse for a few days, but she won't hear of it.''

Nick studied Sam. "I'll take care of it one way or another." Sam opened her mouth to protest, but he cut her off, knowing he was getting so tangled up in Sam's life that he'd have a hell of a time getting free of it when he left. "She won't be alone."

"Good, good. I hear that congratulations are in order for what you did at the courthouse."

Nick nodded, then reached out to take Sam by the arm. She didn't flinch or try to pull back. She let him hold on to her. "We need to go."

"Call if you need me," the doctor said.

Nick nodded again and went outside with Sam. They were almost to the car when a police cruiser came down the street, screeching to a halt beside them. The officer he'd talked to at the courthouse got out and held up the laptop and Sam's purse. "You left these behind."

Nick took them both with his free hand and thanked the officer, who quickly took off again.

Nick tossed the computer and purse into the tiny back seat of the car, eased Sam into the passenger seat, then drove off. When they neared the courthouse, the place was calm, as if nothing had ever happened. He didn't miss the way Sam shifted uneasily and he kept on driving.

Mentally, he sorted out what needed to be done. Get her back to the house, find someone to stay with her, then get out of town. He was so intent on his own thoughts that he was startled when Sam suddenly started speaking in a rush of words.

"I was just coming out of the rest room, and he was there, with…with that gun." He heard her take a shaky breath, and out of the corner of his eye, he saw her nervously wringing her hands. He reacted the way he had the first time, reaching out for her, covering her hands with one of his to still them. "He was so fast, and I couldn't get away. Then you were there, and I can't believe that you just talked to him."

Her hands were trembling, and her words were tumbling out almost faster than she could say them. "I've always…I mean, your job, I never understood, but you're so good at it. You acted as if that man was someone you wanted to help. I mean, you acted as if you cared, as if it was important to you, and he got that. He believed you."

"Win them over," he murmured. "You don't negotiate with someone who hates you."

"Sure, yes, of course, I just never understood…" She took a gulping breath and he held more firmly to her hands.

"Sam, it's over. He's in jail and you're fine." He could feel her tension. "Just breathe slowly. We'll be home soon, and things will look a lot better with some of Mrs. Douglas's soup inside you.''

His heart lurched when he felt her fingers close around his hand and hold on so tightly it made his skin tingle.

## Chapter Thirteen

Nick saw Mrs. Douglas's house come into view, but he couldn't see the elderly lady anywhere before he turned to go to the cottage. As they neared the little house, Sam shifted her hands and he let her go. He stopped the car where he'd parked it before and turned to her.

She sat very still, staring down at her lap. "We're home." He opened his door. "Let's get inside."

He got out, but she didn't move, and he went around the car to her door. He touched her on the shoulder, but she didn't react. She never stopped staring at her lap. "He had a gun, a real gun," she whispered in a strangely flat voice.

"I know, love, it was horrible." She shivered convulsively, and he slid his hand down to hers. "Come on, Sam, please." He opened her door but never let go of her. "Get out of the car."

"He could have killed us," she said, and her

hand moved from his to touch her stomach. "We could have just been gone, as if we had never been. Both of us. Just gone."

He closed his eyes for a moment as the truth of that statement hit him. Sam could have been gone. He reached for her hand again, and she let him take it. She laced her fingers in his, and held on to him with surprising strength. She slowly got out of the car, still clasping his hand as they walked toward the house.

They went through the back door and into the kitchen. At the island, Sam turned to Nick, her grip on him unwavering. Her face was ashen now, the deep green of her eyes too bright against her pale skin. "He kept screaming and screaming, and the police…"

Nick wished he'd asked the doctor for a sedative. Then again, maybe she couldn't take one, being pregnant and all. He was so ignorant about pregnant women it was pathetic. The last thought almost made him laugh. There was no reason for him to know anything about pregnancy, ever. There never would be.

"Oh, Nick," she sighed with a shudder, and he pulled her to him. He couldn't not hold her, or not try to comfort and protect her. She all but collapsed against his chest.

"Sam, it's over," he whispered into her hair.

"Believe me, he's no longer a threat to you. I promise you that."

"You...you said we were married, that the baby..."

He'd said a lot of things. "I said what I had to. I would have told him I could fly if it would have saved you."

The thought of Sam's getting hurt had brought out an almost savage reaction in him, something he hadn't even considered he was capable of until that moment. He would have killed if it meant saving Sam. It was that simple.

"You're going to help him?"

"No, Swicker will. He'll get a fair break." He rubbed his hand up and down on her back, aware of each unsteady breath she took. "Although, if it were up to me, I'd probably just take him out and shoot him."

She pressed her forehead against his chest and started to really sob in earnest. She was shaking all over now, and the only thing he could do was hold on to her. "Oh, Nick...no..."

"Hey, I'm kidding." He kept rubbing slow circles on her back and tried to cut through the intensity of his own feelings with some degree of humor. "Remember who you're talking to. It's me, Nick, the protector of the guilty. The guiltier the better. Remember that everyone has the right to the best defense money can buy. Well, that's me, the attorney without a conscience.''

''Oh, stop,'' she whispered on a soft hiccup, then she drew back and sniffed as she looked up into his face. Her cheeks were tear-streaked, her lashes spiked with moisture, and her chin was far from steady. ''I never said that.''

''Oh, yes, you did. You said it every chance you got.'' He brushed her bottom lip with the ball of his thumb and fought every urge within him to do more than that. His need to get even closer to her was incredible; he felt he had to protect her from every evil in the world. Not kissing her right then was probably the most noble thing he'd ever done in his entire lifetime. He eased her back a bit more and lightly held her by the shoulders. ''You need to eat, love. You need to calm down, forget what happened. It can't be good for you or the baby.''

''I...I don't think I could eat anything.''

''You have to. No more dizzy spells,'' he said, then forced himself to let go of her and cross to the refrigerator. ''I'll heat up that soup for you and see if I can find some crackers, without peanut butter for a change of pace.''

''You said you were leaving,'' she said from across the room.

He turned, the sight of Sam stunning him. ''I lied.'' He knew right then that he wasn't leaving, not now. There was no way he could just walk away, but he had no idea how he could stay. He needed time to figure that one out. At least until she was safe. "I'm here until someone else can be. Now, go and rest, and I'll bring up your food. Then we'll talk."

"Yes, we have to," she said in an unsteady whisper. He heard her go slowly upstairs. He looked at the clock over the refrigerator. They'd been gone less than three hours, but that was enough time for him to realize that Sam was the most important person in his life.

He was startled by a knock on the back door. "Mrs. Douglas?" he said when he opened the door to find the elderly woman standing outside.

"I'm so sorry to bother you like this, but I just heard about that horrible, horrible experience at the courthouse. How is dear Samantha and the baby?"

"Both fine, actually. They're going to be okay."

"It's just wonderful the way you rescued her like that. I mean, the sheriff told me all about it, and it's just…" She gave an exaggerated shudder. "It was absolutely heroic."

"It worked, and that's what counted," he said.

"Is Samantha sleeping?" she asked, looking around him.

"She's resting. Do you want to come in? I'm just heating up the soup you left for her."

"No, no, no, I can't come in. I just stopped by

to make sure she was okay. But you tell her that if she needs anything, I'm here.''

''Mrs. Douglas, I could really use your help.''

''Oh, my dear, anything,'' she said, pressing one hand to her breast.

''Is there any way you could stay with her for a day or two?''

''Oh, dear, I would just love to help out, but Owen is having a very bad time. The tail feathers are gone, and he's starting to pick at his wings. It's just terrible.''

''Could you get someone to sit with him?''

''He's so fragile right now, I really couldn't do that. But if you need more soup, or if you need to talk to someone, you can call on me.''

''Thanks for offering,'' he said.

''So, you'll be staying for a while, then?''

He exhaled. ''Yes, I will be. I might try and find a nurse to hire, but I'll be here until I find someone.''

''I would suggest Maria, but she's got a family of her own. And she's such a gossip. You know.'' She waved one hand vaguely in his direction. ''I mean, you don't need anyone gossiping about this, do you?''

''No, I guess not.''

''Well, good luck. I need to go and give Owen his medicine. The poor thing just hates the medicine. If I put it in his water, he overturns the water holder, and if I put it in his food, he won't eat. Then he gets sick. He's just so bright I can't fool him.''

''Well, Owen is lucky that you're taking care of him,'' he said.

''Just as Samantha is that you are there for her,'' she returned, then patted his arm. ''Bless you, son,'' she said. ''Good evening.''

''Good evening,'' he called after her as she turned and headed out into the night.

He closed the door, at first feeling frustrated by the woman. She was always there, but never there. It was the oddest thing. Then he realized that her refusal to stay with Sam was okay. He wasn't quite ready to leave. Not yet.

WHEN SAM HAD FACED DEATH at the hands of Louis Franco, she experienced one other feeling besides the horrible fear—regret. She could have died and Nick would never have known that the baby she carried was his. And that was her doing. She'd been selfish, not wanting to deal with the truth—looking for the right time. But no time was the right time. The only time she had was now, the present. The future was so unsure. That had been proven to her today in a deadly way.

She had to tell him, and whatever he did or didn't do would be his choice. He had to know before he left, to know that the child he saved today was his own. She had no right to keep it from him any longer. She had never had that right. She'd just thought she did.

As she sat down on the edge of the bed, she knew that there would be no more secrets between them. She stared out the window, at the Pacific in the distance. She didn't know what price there would be to pay when the truth came out, but whatever it was, it wouldn't be nearly as devastating as the price for her lies. She couldn't believe how she'd let him think she had a husband or someone else besides him in her life.

There had only been Nick. Just Nick. Her love. Her only love. She took a shuddering breath and almost jumped when Nick spoke behind her. "You should be lying down."

She took another calming breath, then stood to find him on the other side of the bed with a tray in his hands. "I...I didn't want to. I..." She tried to find the words. "You said we could talk."

"I said after you eat." He put the tray on the table by the bed.

"Nick?" She needed to finally tell him the truth and open up her heart to him. "I have to tell you something. Something that...I should have told you before."

He straightened and slanted a look at her. Then he came around to her side of the bed. Without saying a word, he framed her face with both hands. "Sam, you need to calm down and eat."

She blurted out, "Nick, I could have died."

He was very still, then his thumbs moved slowly on her cheeks. "God, just thinking about that tears me up." His jaw clenched. "I don't know what I would have done. I saw you there and something changed. I don't understand it, but things just…" His voice trailed off, then with a low moan, he leaned closer and his lips found hers.

Every rational thought was gone. His mouth was on hers, his touch explosive and all-encompassing, and every fear that she'd had that day, every pain, was washed away by his touch. There was an aching urgency in the way she wrapped her arms around him, pulling him closer.

Life and death. This was life. She was alive. And she only felt alive when she was in Nick's arms. She wound herself around him, tugging at his shirt, needing to feel his skin under her hands. To hear his heart beat against her cheek, to feel him touch her and find her center, and to give her life meaning. It was that simple and that complicated.

He was tasting her lips, then his mouth feathered over her eyes along to her ear, to a sensitive spot at her throat. Every touch seemed to sear her soul. Every caress made her yearn for more. Gripped by passion, they couldn't seem to let go of each other.

Passion, white-hot and searing, consumed them as they discarded their clothing. Then she was in the bed and Nick was standing by her, the low light etching shadows on his nakedness.

He did nothing to hide the evidence of his desire for her, but he hesitated, his face back in the shadows over her. She wanted him and almost panicked when he didn't touch her again. "Nick," she whispered, holding out her hands to him. "Please?"

He came forward, shifted onto the bed until he was over her but still barely touching her. His heat was everywhere, but the only point of contact was where his thighs touched hers. "Are you sure?" he asked. "Very sure?"

"Please, yes," she gasped. "Please, just for tonight. Just for now."

He lowered himself until his body was lying along hers, her breasts to his chest, his hips pressing against hers, but he didn't take her. Instead, he shifted to one side, his hand skimming over her, finding her breasts, cupping them. His thumb teased her ultrasensitive nipple until she almost cried out from the feelings that flowed through her.

Then his lips replaced his fingers and she arched toward him, willing herself to be closer to this man than was humanly possible. She wanted to lose herself in him, to be folded into his being and never come out. She wanted to love him. And she did. She touched him and explored him…felt him shudder and heard his low moans. As she felt him grow and harden, the give-and-take escalated.

He touched her, and she touched him. He kissed her, and she kissed him. His hand found the inside of her thigh, and she circled his desire with her hand, and arched to his touch when he shook from hers. "Oh, Sam," he moaned, "I've missed you so much." He shifted over her, bracing himself with his hands at either side of her shoulders. And she looked up at him.

"I've missed you," she admitted.

She felt him against her, testing her, and she lifted her hips, inviting his invasion. Then with agonizing slowness, he entered her and filled her, and when he was totally contained inside her, the world stopped. They didn't move, both afraid that if they did, it would be all over. It would be shattered.

Then when Sam couldn't bear to wait any longer, she circled his hips with her legs and moved her hips slowly up to him. He let out a low, almost animal sound, then started to move, matching her actions with his thrusts, and with each stroke, the world fell further and further away.

Sam surged into another place, a place where there was just her and Nick, a place of feeling and pleasure. A place that was theirs alone. The world didn't exist, just the sensations that soared through her, the sense of being one with Nick, of being part of his soul. When the sensations reached a level of almost agonizing ecstasy, she let go.

Every sense was alive, every atom of her body filled with pleasure, and she knew that no matter what happened after this moment, Nick was hers. He'd be in her heart and soul forever, and that would be enough.

NICK DIDN'T EXPECT to have the dream, not when he'd had the reality, but the dream came anyway. Sam and him, together, all tangled up in each other. He could feel every inch of her body against his, every breath she took, then he was stroking her, his need firing up again. He touched her breasts, felt her nipples harden into nubs. His hand lowered, his fingers splaying on her chest, then lower.

That was when the dream shifted. Sam wasn't the same Sam. She had a huge stomach, smoothly round. He felt movement beneath his hand, a kicking against his palm. Sam very pregnant, smiling up at him, telling him the baby would be here soon, that they'd be together, just the three of them. Forever. Forever.

He woke with a start, his skin filmed with cool moisture. The real Sam was snuggled into him, the soft swelling of her stomach fitting neatly against his hip. Her hair tickled his nose, her body pressed into his, angle for angle, her legs tangled in his, and the stillness of night everywhere.

He lay very still, staring up into the shadows, and he wondered what was happening to him. Last night he'd known he wouldn't leave Sam, that he was staying, that there was no way he could have walked out. He'd stay because of the fear in her eyes, the tears that streamed down her cheeks and the need that he felt radiating from her. Because she might have died.

But he'd stayed for himself, out of real selfishness. Something in him wouldn't let him break away and didn't even want to. When she'd come to him, he'd thought it was just for the one night. One more time. To remember her, to burn her image in his heart. He took an unsteady breath. Sometime during the night, everything had changed. Fleeting had changed to lasting. And no matter what happened, he wasn't going to let go the way he had the last time.

She sighed, then moved even closer, and he held on to her, burying his face in her hair and inhaling her essence. Then he felt it, a stirring against his hip—the child. He suspended his breathing for a second until he felt it again, no more than a blip, a butterfly's wing fluttering. But so real.

God, he'd never even thought of children. He'd never planned on having any. He didn't have an ego that needed to be fed by replicating himself, and children were something he didn't want. But even that had changed. From the first time he saw the swelling in Sam's stomach—that suggestion of life—he'd started to feel something else. That's why he'd touched her stomach in the car. It scared him, and it confused him, but a child, this child, was very real.

He closed his eyes, his thoughts tumbling one over the other, confused and crazy. Kids? He held more tightly to Sam. Another man's child? A new life? No, it wasn't possible that he could deal with that. Life couldn't change that much. *He* couldn't change that much. But he knew that the moment he thought Sam might die had changed him. Maybe it changed him more than he thought.

When he felt Sam spread her hand over his heart, he pushed aside his confusion, then she shifted and he looked at her. In the deep shadows, he could tell her eyes were open and a gentle smile touched her lips. ''You awake?'' she whispered.

He touched her cheek, felt its silkiness and tried to hang on to his sanity. All he wanted were answers, but when she touched her lips to his chest, when her tongue ran lightly over his skin, sanity fled. His body responded instantly, tightening, hardening, and when his fingers tangled in her hair, lifting her face to his, he didn't care about anything but Sam.

Passion engulfed him, and despite the fact that

he thought he'd had his fill before, he felt so alone without her. He gathered her to him, tasting the heat of her throat, then the heaviness of her breasts. Her legs straddled him, then she was over him. Her eyes were alive with need, her lips softly parted. Then, as he spanned her waist, she eased down on him and the sense of loneliness was gone.

He slipped deeply into her, into moist heat and silk, and for an eternity, they rested like that. Her over him, her hands on his shoulder, her hair falling forward, her breasts full and heavy. Then she moved. He gasped at the first stroke, then raised his hips toward her, thrusting into her over and over again. Nothing completed him the way Sam did, and in an explosion of shattering pleasure, he finally knew one absolute truth. He knew that love was real, and that love was Sam.

## Chapter Fourteen

Sam slowly drifted awake to hear Nick softly whispering in her ear. She sensed faint light through her eyelids but turned to Nick, letting his heat surround her.

"Sam? I'm going for a swim. How about a morning dip? You and me?" His lips touched the side of her throat. "Coming?"

Although she kept her eyes closed, she was fully conscious. She felt the evidence of their lovemaking in her body, the tenderness of her breasts, the scent of Nick everywhere. "You go," she breathed.

"Are you sure?"

"Yes, go."

"I won't be long. Just stay like that, and I'll be back before you know it."

Then he was gone, and she opened her eyes. The gray light of dawn filtered into the room, a cold light, about as cold as she felt at that moment.

She turned and touched the pillow that still held the imprint of Nick's head, then pulled it toward her and buried her face in it. She inhaled, letting his scent fill her. He'd be back soon, and that would be it. She knew he was going to go, but everything she'd wanted to say last night, but didn't, was still unsaid. No matter what, he had to know. And no matter what, she had last night.

She laid aside the pillow, then got out of bed and crossed to the bathroom. She didn't know how long she stayed in the shower, but when she came out, the light had changed to pink and yellow. She dressed quickly in a loose pink tunic and white overalls. Without bothering about shoes, she started down the stairs.

She went through the silent house to the front door and stepped out onto the veranda. The sky above was clear, but a bank of clouds was rolling in from the ocean. A storm coming, maybe. Something different from the past few days. An omen? She shivered slightly and stepped down onto the coolness of the damp grass.

She half expected to see Nick climbing up the bluff, but there was no one there. Then she heard a sound behind her and turned. He was in the doorway, dressed in jeans, a white shirt unbuttoned and untucked, his hair slicked back from his face. He must have come in while she was in the shower.

Everything about him was exposed by the light,

and her heart literally ached at the sight. What she felt for him went so far beyond love that it had no name. She was thankful for it, saddened by it, and let it sink into her soul to keep forever. She had to hold on to it while she tried to finish what she should have done last night.

"That was fast," she said, staying where she was, keeping that buffer of distance between them.

"I never went. I got downstairs, thought about it, then just took a shower and dressed. I went up to get you, but you weren't there. I knew you'd be out here." He stayed where he was, inclining his head slightly to one side as he studied her. "I was hoping..." His words trailed off as he shrugged. "It's time to talk."

She nodded, hugging herself to still an unsteadiness that was creeping inside her. "Yes, it's time."

He moved across the veranda, then down the steps to stand in front of her. But he didn't touch her. "Have you ever had an epiphany? A moment when all the nonsense made sense? When you realized what life was all about?"

She bit her lip, not about to say that she'd had that every time he touched her and every time the baby moved. "I guess so," she whispered.

"Do you know what? I never had. I mean, all thirty-eight years that I've lived, I've never had a moment of true clarity—until now." He came closer, his hands at his side, and she saw the intensity of his eyes. "Sam, I have to…" He took a breath and shook his head. "God, I knew what I wanted to say two minutes ago. I was positively eloquent in the shower, and now I don't know where to begin."

"Nick, please, before you say anything, I have to tell you something."

He reached out and touched her shoulder, his fingers only lightly resting on her, but even so, robbing her of the ability to speak. "No, me first. I have to get this out or it won't happen. And I've wasted enough time."

"Nick, I—"

He touched her lips with his finger. "Please, let me."

She nodded, then he drew back, breaking their connection completely. "I've been thinking, and I finally figured out why I couldn't leave, why I kept staying even when I had an excuse to get out of here. Why I came up here in the first place. It wasn't the locket and it wasn't because of the dreams."

"Dreams?"

"Never mind. That's not important. What's important is I finally figured out what's happening to me. I want you. I want to be with you. And when Franco was holding that gun on you, threatening to pull the trigger, I realized that I didn't have anything if I didn't have you. I'd have nothing. Nothing.''

Then he touched her cheek lightly with his fingertips and the contact made her tremble.

"Without you, Sam, there's nothing." His voice was low. "And I don't want to live my life like that. I want you and the baby. And if the father ever comes back into the picture..." He drew back. "I can't promise I'll do fatherhood right, but damn it, I'll try. I'll work at it, and you won't be alone with the baby. We'll figure it out. I promise you, we'll make it work."

She heard his words echoing deep inside her. Words that she knew he meant, words that she knew came from his heart. Words that didn't include love. She knew there were tears, but she didn't care. She was holding herself in so tightly she could hardly breathe. "The baby," she whispered.

He took a ragged breath. "I know you've got this guy, and I don't know what your relationship is with him, but he's not here. How much does he care? He wouldn't have left you alone if he cared. Let me deal with him."

"There is no one," she heard herself saying.

"What?"

She bit her lip so hard she was shocked that she didn't taste blood. "No one. Just you."

"What are you talking about?"

"You, Nick, you." She pressed her hands to her stomach, and the baby moved. It pressed against her hands, but she didn't look away from Nick. "You're the father."

"Sam, don't. We can't make believe no matter how much either one of us wishes that things were different."

"That night you were so sick, and I was there, and you..." She shrugged as if it could ease some of the tension inside her, but it didn't help, not when he was staring at her as if she had lost her mind. "You and I, we were in the living room, and I just kissed you, just to say goodbye, and the next thing..." She swiped at tears that wouldn't stop. "We...we..."

He obliterated any distance between them, coming within inches and grinding out words. "You're telling me we slept together that night?"

She nodded.

"Good God," he muttered. She saw him take a ragged breath. "And I was so drunk or so drugged that I thought...I thought it was a dream? You're telling me that we slept together and you just walked out and never said a word to me?"

"Nick, we were divorced," she managed to get out.

"Divorced? Did you sign the papers before or after we made love?" he demanded.

"After."

He gestured at her stomach, a sharp motion that almost made her flinch. ''And that…the baby, that happened that night? There was no other man, no guy you jumped into bed with after you left me?''

His anger fueled her own, and her feeling of desperation that had been growing as she tried to tell him the truth was being pushed aside by that anger. ''I didn't jump into bed with anyone but you,'' she said, her voice louder now.

''You've been lying all this time? You let me believe that there was some guy lurking out there, some jerk who didn't want a baby and walked out on you!''

''I never called you a jerk,'' she muttered. ''But you didn't want a baby and you sure as hell didn't want me, did you?''

The question hung between them, and nothing could take it back or change the truth in it. Nick didn't deny it or even attempt to answer. He just stared at her, then without another word, he turned and walked away from her into the house.

Sam screamed after him, ''Don't you walk away like that! I'm not finished!''

He turned back to her, the sun exposing the way his jaw was working and the anger in his eyes. ''I thought you were.''

''Not yet.''

''What?''

''That's it? You say all that stuff about needing

me and working this out, then you're walking away? You're leaving?'' She swiped at the tears, the pain overwhelming her, but she couldn't stop. ''And you wonder why I didn't tell you about the baby before? What would you have done back then? Insist on an abortion? Left the country to get away? Why would I have told you? I regret telling you now.''

Nick felt the world exploding. He'd had the future all set when he stepped out of the shower. He'd had it all centered and sane. Now insanity was there in spades and he wanted nothing more than to go someplace to find peace. To figure out his life.

No, he'd tried that before by coming here. And it hadn't worked. He stared at Samantha, at the tears on her face she was ignoring and the way her jaw was set. God, he loved her. That thought rocked him to the core. A reality that wouldn't be denied. A love that was mixed with pain and confusion and need and desire. But love. And he couldn't walk away.

He went toward her, not touching her, but close enough. ''Sam, I'm not doing this right, I know that. I've never done it before.''

''You made sure you never did. You never wanted children. I know that, Nick, and you don't have to do anything about this baby. I just felt you had to know. I should have told you before, but I was so afraid, and now this is all a horrible mess.''

His heart broke for her, for what he'd done to her. He'd never even known he was capable of hurting anyone the way he'd hurt her. He reached out and gently brushed at her tears. ''Shhh, please stop. Please.''

She took a shuddering breath. ''Just go. It's okay. I'll manage.''

''Sam, I'm not going. I'd never make it out your door. I'd keep coming back. I'd have to.''

She stared at him, wide-eyed. ''What do you mean?''

He drew back. ''Listen to me, because I'm going to say something that I've never said to another person in my life. Never. Do you understand that?''

She nodded.

''Okay, here goes. I love you, Samantha. I've loved you from the moment I saw you in that courtroom, and I've loved you every minute since then. The thing is, I'm so stupid, so dense, that I didn't even know it was love until now.

''The only love I saw in my life had a life span of three years and ended with divorce papers, and this was repeated over and over again. But I never knew that there really was love, that there was an emotion that came to you when you least expected it and made another person the most important thing in the world. I never knew…until now.''

He stood in front of her, having revealed more about himself than he'd ever done before in his entire life. He'd laid bare his soul to her, and she was just standing there, staring at him, saying nothing.

Then she took a breath and whispered, ''The baby?''

''You're right. I never wanted kids. Never. But that was because I never met anyone I wanted to be with, anyone I wanted to spend the rest of my life with. Because when I thought of kids, I thought of military school and boarding school and parents who lived in different countries and hated each other.''

''And now?''

''I found you.'' He touched her then, unable to keep his hands off her any longer. He touched her shoulders, then slid his hands up her throat to frame her face. ''Tell me I'm not too late. Tell me that you don't hate me and that you'll let me into your life. I don't have one without you, you know. None.''

Sam had never known pure happiness in her life. She'd never felt as if she really belonged anywhere, even here. But in that moment, she found a home. She went into Nick's arms and just held on to him. The world stabilized and steadied. It felt solid and sure under her feet. She had her anchor. Nick.

She held him close, then felt the baby kick, and she knew that Nick felt it, too, when he whispered, "Another constituent heard from?"

"Oh, yes," she breathed.

His hands framed her face again and his expression was intense. "This can work, can't it?"

"I hope so. But your work…I don't want to live in Los Angeles and you have your practice there, and…" It was getting complicated already.

"I worked that out in the shower, too. How do you feel about half and half?"

"What?"

"Live in Malibu part of the time and live up here the rest. I've got my first client, Louis Franco. He needs help and he's guilty as hell. My type of client—at least I can help Swicker with it."

"Do you mean that?"

"Absolutely, except for one thing."

She felt her breath catch. "What?"

"Could you…would you love me?"

"Oh, Nick, I told you when you asked me why I slept with the baby's father. I told you I did it because I loved him." His hands trembled on her. "I love you, Nicholas." She threw back her head and yelled, "I love Nicholas Viera! I love my husband!"

"Oh, my dears, that's wonderful."

They were both startled and turned. Still holding on to each other, they saw Mrs. Douglas coming out of the trees. The elderly lady was in her usual jeans and loose shirt, but no hat. This time, she had a scraggly gray bird that looked like a plucked chicken on her shoulder. Owen. She lifted a hand in greeting as she came across the lawn toward them.

"Good morning," she said.

"We didn't know you were here," Nick admitted.

"I heard you both from my yard," she returned, smiling at the two of them.

Nick pulled Sam tightly to his side, and she held on to him, not about to let him go even for a minute. "I'm sorry."

"Oh, no, don't apologize. It's so good to see two truly happy people around here." The bird picked at her hair, but she paid it no notice. "I had hopes that you loved our Samantha, that you just didn't know it, and I was right."

"You were very right. A wise woman," Nick said.

She came closer and touched Nick on his arm. "So, what are your intentions for Samantha and the little one?"

"We need to get married, then we'll play it by ear. But we'll do it together."

"Can I do anything for you two? Help with the wedding? Baby-sit when the little one comes?"

Nick laughed at that. "We'll figure that out when the time comes. For now, why don't you take Owen home, look after him, and I'll look after Sam."

She smiled at him. "Do you mean that?"

"Absolutely."

"Good man," she said fervently, then turned to the bird. "Owen, let's go home. It's medicine time." The bird squawked as the elderly lady headed off across the grass. "Oh, by the way, if you want to go swimming, I can't see a thing from my house," she called, then disappeared into the trees.

Nick turned to Sam and they both burst out laughing, still in each other's arms. Then Sam sobered and looked up at Nick. "How about that swim?"

"I still don't have a suit," he said with a wicked grin.

"Mrs. Douglas says she can't see a thing from her house." She reached up and kissed him. But when she caught his intense gaze, she knew she wasn't interested in going to the beach.

"We'll swim later," he said in a low, rough voice. "I've got something else in mind right now."

Sam put her arm around Nick and returned to the cottage with him. They stepped inside, and Sam knew that for the first time in her life, she had a home, a real home. With Nick.

# *Epilogue*

*A year later*

The Jensen Pass art gallery was the center of the small town's social world. On this evening, the gallery was awash with crystal, roses and magical paintings. The patrons, mostly locals with a few out-of-town critics, wandered through a myriad of displays, drinking chilled champagne and nibbling on chocolates. Dr. Barnet, in a tuxedo, was escorting his wife, a small, round woman who was wearing a lavender gown. Maria was there with her husband, a burly man who, Nick knew, drove a truck.

Nick looked across the room at Sam. His wife never ceased to amaze him, her beauty blinding him. She fairly glittered in a shimmering silver dress, her longer hair piled on top of her head and caught with diamond clips. It had been her idea to have the showing here. And it was working. The paintings were of local scenes and filled with life.

He glanced at the painting she'd finished in those first days they were together again—the child coming out of the surf. But she'd made revisions to it, changing the painting months later to have the face of the child resemble their child.

He shifted his daughter in his arms, pleased she had her mother's pale hair and deep green eyes. "Your mommy's doing a good job," he said. Seven-month-old Jensen Samantha Viera looked up at her daddy and reached out to grab at the red carnation stuck in the lapel of Nick's tuxedo. "Hey, no. No good to eat," he said.

Someone placed a hand on his shoulder and he turned around to see Greg. The tall, lean redhead grinned at him. "I never thought I'd see the day," he said.

"Sam deserves it," Nick said, trying to spot his wife across the room.

"Not that. It's obvious she's got talent. I'm talking about you. Nicholas Viera, the father, the husband. What a long, strange trip it's been."

Very long and very strange, and very wonderful. He shifted Jensen, letting her fiddle with the studs on his shirt. "It was a shock, that's for sure."

"No regrets?" Greg asked.

"Oh, yeah, lots of those, but none since I came to my senses."

"She's drooling."

"What?"

"The baby, she's drooling all over your jacket," Greg said, taking out a handkerchief and holding it out to Nick.

Before Nick could wipe at his jacket, Jensen snatched the handkerchief, giggling as she waved it in the air. "Thanks for the toy," the proud father said to Greg.

Nick looked around the room again, needing to see Sam. A strange phenomenon had begun a year ago and he always craved the sight of her.

He turned back to Greg, but the lawyer had moved away and Sam was standing there instead. He smiled at her, and Jensen dived for her mommy. Sam scooped the child into her arms, then looked at Nick over the child's head as the baby snuggled into her mother's chest. "Do you think it would be rude if we left?"

"It's your show. What do you think?"

She leaned toward him. "I want to be with you, and Mrs. Douglas has offered to take Jensen to Doc Malone's to show her the monkey the vet just got."

"So that means we have the house to ourselves?"

She grinned at him. "That means we have the beach to ourselves. Even better."

All she had to do was look at him, and the

dreams were a reality. ''Good idea,'' he said, then
started over to Mrs. Douglas. In a few minutes, he
and Sam were slipping out the back door, heading
for his convertible. ''I'm driving,'' he said with a
grin, and moments later they were heading toward
the cottage. He reached for her hand. ''Suits or no
suits?'' he asked.

''Well, Mrs. Douglas won't be around, so I'm
voting for no suits.''

He stepped on the accelerator when he spotted
the driveway ahead. Her parked by the cottage, and
lifted Sam into his arms, carrying her over the
grass and toward the bluffs. It was twilight, the sky
streaked with vivid colours.

When they got to the edge of the bluffs, Nick
set Sam on her feet and, keeping ahold of her hand,
led the way down to the beach. Without speaking,
they undressed each other and hand in hand they
raced into the water together.

Their kiss was explosive, and her hands on him
brought an instant response. Her legs circled his
waist, then as they slipped below the water's surface, he entered her. The experience was other-
worldly, unimaginably sensual. And he knew he
wanted more.

He left her, turning and motioning to the shore.
They stumbled out of the water and crossed the
sands to where they'd left towels and toys in the

shelter of the rocks. Nick grabbed the towel, laid it out on the sand and reached for Sam.

She came to him, and they tumbled onto the towel. He wanted it to last forever, but as soon as he entered her, all his patience vanished. He filled her and he knew her, and even if they lived to be a hundred, he'd never have enough of her. Sam rose to meet him thrust for thrust, and the moment of completion came in a rush, an earth-shattering barrage of ecstasy that only got better with time.

Sam was in his arms, her cheek against his heart, and she sighed "A short swim," she whispered.

"We have time, love, we have time," he said. "We have a lifetime."

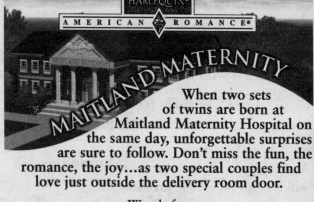